Christmas at Grace Hollow

CHAD MUESSIG

CHAD MUESSIG
B O O K S

CHRISTMAS AT GRACE HOLLOW

Book Cover by Chad Muessig

ISBN 979-8-9989994-3-7 (paperback)

ISBN 979-8-9989994-5-1 (ebook)

Library of Congress Control Number:

First Edition October 2025

Published by Chad Muessig Books

Vineland, NJ

@ChadMuessigBooks

For my children...
Though you are scattered around the world, you are never far from my heart. At Christmas, remember that no matter where you are, you will always have a place to call home.

Playlist

I'll Be Home for Christmas	Rascal Flatts
Go Tell it on the Mountain	MercyMe
Last Christmas	Wham!
Do You Hear What I Hear?	Whitney Houston
All I Want for Christmas is You	Mariah Carey
Rockin' Around The Christmas Tree	Brenda Lee
Do They Know It's Christmas? 1984	Band Aid
Blue Christmas	Elvis Presley
O Come, All Ye Faithful	Pentatonix
Baby, It's Cold Outside	Frank Sinatra
Angels We Have Heard On High	for KING&COUNTRY
While You Were Sleeping	Casting Crowns
O Holy Night	Josh Groban
Silent Night	Carrie Underwood
Noel - Live	Chris Tomlin
All is Well	Michael W. Smith
Please Come Home for Christmas	Eagles
Hark! The Herald Angels Sing	Pentatonix
O Come, O Come, Emmanuel	Lauren Daigle
White Christmas	Bing Crosby
What Child is This? - Live	Chris Tomlin, All Sons...
The Heart of Christmas	Matthew West

One

Snowflakes dance and twirl around my rented Jeep Wrangler as I cautiously steer onto Main Street. The tires emit a satisfying crunch as they press through a thin, compacted layer of snow that blankets the road. Through the frosty windshield, Maple Ridge materializes like a postcard from the past, as if it's been patiently waiting for my return all these years. I lower the window, and a brisk gust of air rushes in, nipping at my cheeks and carrying with it the crisp, invigorating scent of pine and wood smoke. The Christmas lights strung across the quaint storefronts twinkle like a constellation of tiny stars, casting a warm, festive glow. I force myself to concentrate on these cheerful decorations, trying to push aside the flood of memories they evoke. *Just breathe, Tess.*

The drive from the airport had been like slipping through time. With every mile, the chaos of New York faded a little more—the honking taxis, the neon glare, the constant hum of motion replaced by open skies and the quiet majesty of snow-dusted evergreens. The two-lane road wound through familiar hills, each turn revealing pieces of my past I hadn't realized I'd missed—the rusted fence of old ranch land, the weathered red barn that always leaned a little too far east, the frozen river glinting like glass in the fading light. It was as if the land itself remembered me, whispering pieces of who I used to be before ambition and heartbreak drove me away. And as Maple Ridge came into view, framed by the distant mountains and the soft glow of dusk, I couldn't help wondering if I'd ever truly left it behind—or if some part of me had been waiting all these years to come home.

Only weeks before Christmas, Maple Ridge welcomes me like an old friend whose embrace I'm not quite ready to return. As I navigate through its snow-dusted streets, each familiar building evokes a flood of memories that are both comforting and unsettling. The corner bakery, adorned with a festive holly wreath, instantly transports me back to those chilly morning when I would dash inside to grab a warm, gooey cinnamon bun before heading to school. The hardware store, its façade glowing warmly under a cascade of blinking lights, stands unchanged since my childhood. I can almost hear the nostalgic jingle of the bell above the door, recalling the times my friends and I would scurry inside, seeking refuge from the biting cold. Everything appears so unchanged, so familiar. Each recognizable sight tightens the knot in my stomach, whispering that the ghosts of my past might still linger here, refusing to vanish as I once hoped they would.

I attempt to dismiss the all-too-familiar feeling that hangs over me like an overcast sky. I'm haunted by the worry that those who once knew me might still carry the wounds left by my past self. A quick glance at the dashboard reveals the illuminated clock, its harsh glow serving as a stark reminder of the choice I've made and my need to follow through with it.

As I turn onto the familiar street, a lone snowflake drifts lazily from the sky, landing gently on my windshield and melting away with a slow, deliberate grace, leaving behind a glistening trail like that of a wandering tear. At Cottonwood Path's end, my childhood home stands proudly, adorned with Christmas lights that wrap snugly around the porch rails and bushes, casting a warm, twinkling glow against the evening's chill. An inflatable Santa Claus, larger than life, stands sentinel in the yard, his jolly presence adding a whimsical touch to the scene. My hands clutch the steering wheel tighter, my knuckles turning a stark white as I summon the courage to steer into the driveway. I turn off the engine, and the sudden silence envelops me like a thick blanket, my breath hanging in the air, a soft rhythm in the stillness.

The day I left is etched in my memory as if it were only yesterday. Mom, tears streaming down her face. Dad, his voice a quiet promise to pray for me. I had sworn to myself then that I would never return, that I would move forward without looking back. But seeing Mom's face on the screen—the worry etched around her eyes, the way her voice trembled when she said Dad "isn't doing well"—pulls at me with a fierce urgency. She's asked me to come home before, more times than I can count, but this time is different. There's something in her expression, something unspoken, that grips my chest and won't let go. The weight of everything left unsaid between us, between Dad and me, made it impossible to tell her no.

I sneak a peek at my phone, half praying for an excuse to start the engine and speed off. Nothing. No missed calls. No messages. Just the blank screen mirroring my own wavering gaze. With a resigned exhale, I set it aside, snatch my bag, and swing open the car door. The biting chill rushes in, wrapping me in its icy grip. My heart thunders against my ribcage as I trudge towards the house, each step feeling as if I've strapped lead weights to my sneakers - or 'tennis shoes' as they're known here at home - anchoring me against any instinctual urge to bolt in fear.

I halt at the bottom step of the porch, watching my breath form tiny clouds in the cold air. Just as I'm about to run, the door slowly opens with a creak. Stuck in that moment, it feels like time is expanding endlessly before me, reflecting the long years I've been gone.

"Tess!" My mother's voice calls out to me, full of warmth against the chill of the evening air.

There she is, standing in the doorway, a familiar silhouette against the warm light spilling from inside the house. Her smile is as radiant as the twinkling Christmas lights lining the porch behind her. She wears a blue cable-knit sweater, just like the one she knitted during those long winter evenings when I was in high school. Even her jeans are tucked into worn leather boots just like the kind she'd wear to my soccer games, standing on the sidelines in all weather. The porch light catches the silver strands in her hair, illuminating her face—the same face that used to peek into my bedroom to whisper goodnight long after she thought I was asleep. Over the years, that same face has appeared in countless video calls—birthdays, holidays, and those brief check-ins where we both smiled a little too brightly, pretending the distance between us didn't matter.

Before I can even process it all, she's rushing down those steps and pulling me into a hug., wrapping me in the scent of her favorite perfume—a fragrance I'd almost forgotten but now recognize with surprising clarity.

I'd promised myself no tears, but they betray me, spilling hot and unbidden down my cold cheeks. Despite this, I force a smile, feeling it strain against the weight of all the words I can't bring myself to say. Wrapping my mom in a hug, I cling to her like I'm terrified of letting go.

"Oh, hun," Mom murmurs, her grip tightening around me. "It's so good to see you."

Swallowing hard against the lump in my throat, I nod into her shoulder. "It's good to see you too, Mom," I manage to whisper back.

I pull back, searching my mom's face for clues. Is that relief I see? Joy? Shock? It's hard to tell through the blur of my own tears.

"Come on in before you turn into a snowman," Mom chides with a laugh that has the familiar warmth of a gentle reprimand. She hooks her arm through mine, guiding me up the steps and across the threshold.

A wave of heat greets us as we step inside, enveloping me so suddenly it makes my head spin. Everything is just as I remember it: the same family portraits gracing the walls, holiday cards bordering the door frame like festive wallpaper. The air carries that unmistakable scent of Christmas—freshly baked cookies mingling with pine needle aroma. Mom helps me shrug off my coat and then pauses, cradling my face in her hands.

"You're really here," Mom murmurs, her eyes bright with unshed tears. "I wasn't sure..."

"Neither was I," I confess, a shaky laugh escaping my lips. My fingers trace the corners of my eyes, attempting to regain some semblance of control.

"Frank!" She calls into the depths of our old dining room. "She's here!" The sound of Dad's name sends a fresh wave of anxiety washing over me. I draw in a deep breath, steeling myself as I trail behind Mom deeper into the house. With each step, the ghosts from my past and fears for an uncertain future press in on me, threatening to consume me whole.

A dull throb pulses in my chest as I take in the uncanny stillness of this place. It's an odd sensation, like stepping into a photograph of a past life - so strange, yet painfully familiar. The aroma of oatmeal cookies wafts from the kitchen, mingling with the sharp scent of evergreen from the lavishly decorated tree nestled in the corner.

My mother guides me towards the entryway, her voice a soothing drone as she speaks. "Can't believe how long it's been," Mom murmurs, her voice soft as a lullaby, her gaze fixed on me. She's got that motherly worry in her eyes, and I feel a pang of guilt. "You must have so many questions, sweetheart."

I give a noncommittal shrug, my words catching in my throat. "Didn't know if I could do it...if I could come back," I confess, fighting to keep the tremor out of my voice. "But I was worried about Dad."

Mom shakes her head, that ever-present smile still dancing on her lips. "You're here now, and that's all that matters."

Her kindness stings like saltwater in a fresh wound and tears prick at the corners of my eyes again. Blinking rapidly, I push them back - *I gotta be strong.* It surprises me how quickly the old balance between vulnerability and defiance can be picked up again.

"Things aren't exactly how you left them," Mom says, her gaze soft yet holding something I can't quite decipher. "But they haven't changed as much as you would think."

I try to offer a smile, though it feels brittle and paper-thin. "That's exactly what scares me."

A silence stretches between us, the comforting warmth of the house seeping into my chilled bones. It's almost enough to dissolve my anxiety. Almost.

"You must be famished after your flight and drive," Mom interjects, deftly steering the conversation away from dangerous territory. "Dinner's ready if you're up for it."

I hesitate, the fear of being home, of confronting everything I've left behind, surges in my chest once more. But against Mom's hopeful expression, resistance proves futile. "Sounds good," I manage to say, my voice finding some stability.

Mom wraps me in another hug, not as desperate as the first, but just as heartfelt. "Let's get you fed, then."

I trail behind her into the dining room, each step a tiny victory over the doubts that continue to cast their shadows around my heart.

The door between the dining room and kitchen creaks open, and my gaze locks with a figure I've only seen occasionally on a screen for years—his presence somehow both familiar and startlingly real in the warm light of home. Dad, standing there like he's bracing for a storm. His face hasn't changed much, still framed by that meticulous salt-and-pepper hair.

"Tess," he says, his voice steady but touched with a weariness I don't remember. His hand drifts to the front of his neatly pressed shirt, fingers brushing the fabric as if grounding himself in the moment.

"Dad." My reply is barely above a whisper, yet it lingers in the air between us like an echo refusing to fade away.

He hesitates before finally stepping into the room, pulling out the chair across from me with a soft scrape against the wooden floor.

He slides into his chair, barely glancing my way. "I didn't expect you'd be back so soon," he murmurs after a beat, his eyes fixed on the gleaming tabletop.

"I didn't expect to be back at all," I reply softly, with a faint edge that makes the words half-serious, half-teasing. The tension between us hangs in the air like an unspoken joke—familiar, sharp, and as old as our history.

Just then, Mom bustles in from the kitchen, her energy nudging away some of the heavy silence that's settled over us. As we start our meal in near silence, she tries to lift our spirits with stories about Maple Ridge—its unchanging storefronts and annual Christmas decorations.

"And you know," Mom mentions offhandedly as she hands me the bowl of mashed potatoes. "We have a pretty big Christmas program at Grace Hollow Community Church."

My heart stutters in my chest at her words. "That's nice," I manage to murmur, the past suddenly looming too large and too close. *Always about church.*

Across the table, Dad watches me, his expression quiet and reserved. I feel both the comfort of familiarity and the unease of distance—as if I've returned to a place I know, but through eyes that no longer see me the same way. His nod earlier caught me off guard, and though it was warmer than I expected, I can't tell if it was genuine or simply polite. Unsure, I lower my gaze, letting the soft glow of the candle in the center of the table hold my attention instead.

"Mom, this is delicious," I say, forcing a brightness into my tone that doesn't quite light up my eyes. Mom's face brightens at my words, her smile radiating warmth that somehow seeps through the heavy atmosphere in the room.

"I hoped you'd enjoy it. I made your favorite, sweetheart. Couldn't let your first night back go by without a little celebration."

My gaze drops to the table, taking in the plate of breaded pork chops, creamy mashed potatoes and the green beans before me. The sight of it pulls at something deep inside - a sudden twinge of nostalgia for these familiar home-cooked meals I'd left far behind.

A hesitant smile tugs at my lips, as delicate and precarious as thin ice on the brink of cracking. The warmth of this moment catches me off guard - not just from Mom's home-cooked meal, but also from the simple joy found in sharing it with family. Dad sits silently at the far end of the table, his quiet demeanor casting a long, unspoken shadow across our snug dining room. The steady tick-tock of the wall clock punctuates our conversation, each tick echoing loudly in my head - a constant reminder of every second I've spent away from this place that was once my home.

"Dad, how's the practice these days?" I ask, keeping my tone casual, though there's an undercurrent of testing the waters. We've talked about it before—I know how busy he is—but I want to hear it from him now, to gauge how he's really doing. He shrugs, eyes drifting past me to something over my shoulder.

"And your work in New York?" he counters, his voice carrying a practiced neutrality that feels deliberate.

"It's good," I say carefully, choosing my words. "Busy, but good." My voice carries just enough warmth to keep it light, though inside I'm watching him closely.

His nod is brief but measured, settling between us like a quiet punctuation in our conversation. The silence that follows feels soft but heavy with unspoken words. I trace lazy circles through the potatoes on my plate, letting the stillness linger just a moment longer.

It dawns on me that dad and I are both healers. He has been Maple Ridge's trusted doctor for as long as I can recall; his name a beacon of comfort for many. And yet here I am, treading along the same path but uncertain whether he sees my journey as progress or missteps.

I've always been in awe of my dad's steadfast dedication to the medical field, his talent for soothing fears and mending injuries. Yet, beneath his stern exterior, I constantly wrestle with doubt—does he truly feel proud of my career path, or does he view it as a disappointment? This journey we embarked on together was supposed to bring us closer, but instead, it feels like an ever-widening chasm.

Mom's soft cough pulls me back into the moment, her gaze shifting between Dad and me. "And your apartment, Tess? Still the same?" she asks, her tone gentle but carrying the weight of knowing—I've shown her the place on video calls enough times for her to picture it.

I nod, grateful for a question that feels safe to answer. "Yeah," I say, my voice steadier than I feel. "Nothing new. No major renovations. But…" My words falter as I search for a way to finish without revealing truths I'm not ready to admit. Mom's expectant look nudges me forward. "But it doesn't feel like home," I confess softly, meeting her eyes.

The unspoken truth hangs heavy in the air between us - not daring to hint to dad about why I'm here now, so unexpectedly. Dad squirms in his chair across from me, his jaw tightening ever so slightly - a telltale sign of his discomfort. A wave of concern washes over me as my thoughts race towards his health - a topic that terrifies me to even consider broaching. Part of me is desperate for reassurance while another part fears that truth might be more devastating than my worst nightmares.

"The place isn't so bad, you know," I rush to add, hoping to lighten the heaviness that my admission has dropped into the room. Mom reaches out and gives my hand a comforting squeeze. "I'm sure it is, sweetheart."

The rest of dinner unfolds more in silence than in talk. The clinks and scrapes of silverware become a makeshift conver- sation in the void left by our inability to find words. My heart pounds a relentless rhythm against my ribcage, and even the sound of my own chewing seems amplified.

I cast an indirect look at Dad, wishing I had some way to decode his thoughts or get a glimpse into what he's feeling. Does he want me gone already? Each time I attempt to voice my thoughts; words stick stubbornly in my throat. So instead, I stay silent, letting the steady ticking of the clock fill up the room. It feels like an echo of all my uncertainties - each tick another reminder of just how long it's been since I last sat at this table.

Mom's voice masterfully steers our conversation in a new direction. "The town's been buzzing with all these holiday events. It's almost hard to keep up."

I nod, though I already know what she means. Every year, without fail, she has told me about how Maple Ridge transforms for Christmas—its heart shifting into something out of a storybook. The town square becomes a wonderland, with twinkling lights strung between lampposts, wreaths draped over every storefront, and a towering tree at the center, crowned with glowing ornaments. Wooden stalls line the square, offering handmade crafts and steaming mugs of cider, while carolers and musicians fill the air with cheerful songs. It's a tradition that turns the whole town into a sort of North Pole, and though my memories of it are fleeting and I've heard about it countless times over the years.

There's something about knowing it's happening now that stirs a quiet longing in me. "I saw the decorations," I say, "Everything looks just as it did when I left."

Mom chuckles softly at my observation. "Well, you know Maple Ridge. We don't like change."

"I guess not," I agree, my words laced with both warmth and an undercurrent of something less sweet. How I wish some things could have remained untouched by time, preserved like cherished Christmas ornaments.

"And the church has been thriving," Mom continues, her voice brightening as she latches onto a topic she hopes will engage me. "You wouldn't believe all the changes."

"Really?" I manage to choke out, straining to lace my words with a hint of excitement. Finding common ground with their world of faith and devotion feels like an uphill battle. I'm on the outside looking in at a life that used to be mine. There was a time when church and the Bible were woven into the fabric of my everyday existence. My parents held them close to their hearts, and as a young girl, I mirrored their reverence. Fragments of youth group memories drift through my mind—the faint scent of coffee and snacks, the hum of acoustic guitar strumming, and the sound of laughter bouncing off bright-painted walls.

But time has a way of carrying you away whether you're ready or not. I ran from the past, and in that flight, my focus shifted—science became my refuge, medicine my anchor. The hospital replaced the church; lab coats and stethoscopes replaced Sunday dresses and Bibles. Now, looking back at the world I left behind feels like watching someone else's life pass by on a film reel—familiar in fragments, but distant and altered.

Dad breaks the silence this time, his voice calm but carrying its usual quiet firmness. "Brayden's been doing well since he took over. Wouldn't you agree, Susan?" He glanced toward Mom with a steady, thoughtful look, be-traying little else.

My fork drops against my plate, the sound sharper than I expect. My breath catches. "Brayden?" I whisper, disbelief threading my voice. "Brayden James?"

"He's the pastor now," Mom says softly, her eyes shift-ing to me with an expression I can't quite read. "Took over a some years back at Grace Hollow."

I blink, stunned. We video chat and talk fairly of-ten—enough that I thought I'd know if something like this had happened. "But... you never told me," I say quietly, my voice trembling. "We talk. We video chat. How did I not know?"

Dad shifts in his seat, meeting my gaze with that same calm reserve. "We tried," he says plainly. "But it never felt like the right time."

Mom gives a faint, almost apologetic nod. "I thought you knew. I thought we'd mentioned it in passing."

My chest tightens, the weight of the revelation settling over me like a sudden winter storm. My eyes dart between them, searching for more—answers, intention, something. But all I find is the quiet between us, heavier than ever. I force a breath past the lump in my throat. "I didn't know," I murmur again, though the words feel too small to hold the storm inside me.

The silence falls again but it's different this time - heavy with unspoken thoughts and feelings stirred up by this revelation. Brayden's name lingers in the air between us like an unwanted guest, resurrecting memories from our shared past and casting their long shadows over our present moment.

The room seems to shrink around me as I recoil, my mind a whirlwind of images and questions. How could Brayden still be here, still woven into the fabric of their lives? How much has he changed? Or has he not changed at all? *He's a Pastor?*

My mother's voice, soft as a lullaby, attempts to anchor me back to reality. "He's done so much for the community. People really look up to him."

I nod in response, but her words barely penetrate the fog of my thoughts. All I can focus on is our last encounter, the unspoken words that hung heavily between Brayden and me. My return to Maple Ridge suddenly feels like a mountain climb rather than a simple homecoming.

The soft scrape of wood against wood draws me out of my thoughts as Dad rises from the table. "I'll get the coffee," he says gently, his tone carrying a quiet, familiar finality.

As I watch him leave, an ache settles in my chest; it's clear he needs space from more than just our dinner table. Turning towards Mom, I find her gaze filled with worry, empathy and something that resembles hope.

"I'm sorry," I manage to choke out. "I didn't mean to..."

She cuts me off with a comforting squeeze of my hand and shakes her head gently. "It's a lot to take in. I know."

Drawing in a shaky breath, I feel the walls closing in further and the air growing denser by the second. "I thought he left," I whisper mostly to myself.

"Brayden's gone through his own transformations," Mom says softly, her tone gentle. "Perhaps, in time, you'll see for yourself."

Her words send my heart into a frantic rhythm. The instinct to bolt, to escape and abandon everything, washes over me like a tidal wave. But there's something else too; a yearning to understand, to witness firsthand what time has done to the people and places I believed were lost forever.

"Tess, are you okay?" Mom asks gently, her gaze scanning my face for signs of distress.

I nod in response even though "okay" feels like a distant concept at this point. I attempt a smile but it quivers on my lips. "I will be," I manage to say, the words sounding more like an oath to myself than anything else.

Mom pulls me into another hug, her presence serving as a soothing anchor amidst the storm of emotions raging within me. "One step at a time, sweetie," she advises softly, her voice wrapping around my frayed nerves like a warm blanket.

The past and present collide in the silent room creating an intoxicating blend that leaves me feeling both rattled and oddly determined. The clock continues its steady march forward, indifferent to the emotional turmoil unfolding beneath its watchful gaze. Dad returns with cups of steaming coffee, and we fall into an awkward yet familiar dance of reacquainting ourselves with each other's company.

Two

Later, I quietly slip out the back door, shooting a glance over my shoulder as I button up my coat against the night's chill. My parents believe it's best if I stay in for the night, that I'm not ready for the memories that might ensnare me like tangled Christmas lights. But I'm not a girl anymore and I need to see what has changed; or what hasn't. The house sits silent behind me, it's warm light spilling onto the snow-covered porch. Tucking my hands into my pockets I take a deep breath, feeling the air crisp and biting in my lungs. Stepping onto the icy pavement, my boots crunch softly in a rhythm that echoes with the gentle fall of snowflakes catching in my auburn hair. My journey down this quiet street takes me deeper into Maple Ridge's heart and closer to a past I've tried so hard to forget.

The stubborn, unchanging brick walls of my old school build- ing loom large as I walk. The sight yanks me back to those late nights sneaking out with Brayden, his eyes ablaze with mischief and his leather jacket casually slung over one shoulder. We'd race down the hill, intoxicated by the thrill of breaking rules, our laughter tangling with the crisp night air as we left the world in our wake. I pause for a moment now, letting the icy wind coil around me, watching as memories play out in vibrant flashes. Back then, I was someone else - carefree and reckless. Someone I'm not sure I'd even recognize now.

The sight of a lone police car parked along the curb pulls me from my memories. Its engine purrs softly, cut- ting through the silence of the night. I'm taken back to those days when Brayden and I would scramble for cover after skipping school, our hearts racing with adrena- line-fueled excitement. In my mind, I can almost see the officer inside that car now, struggling against heavy eye- lids in the yawning quiet of this small-town evening. As I cross the town square, the towering Christmas tree grabs my attention, its branches sagging under the weight of ornaments and years of tradition. A soft melody wafts through the air towards me - "White Christmas" by Bing Crosby. I pause, the music stirring up memories of a past Christmas dance and the scandal that unfolded soon after. The shocked and disappointed faces of my parents flash in my mind, but I quickly shove them back into the recesses as I press on. The night sprawls out ahead of me, each street bathed in festive lights echoing remnants of who I once was and what I left behind.

Main Street is awash with nostalgic glow; storefronts adorned with holiday cheer. As I drift past the diner, hours spent tucked away in its back booth flood back to me - Brayden's hands cradling a steaming cup of coffee, his infectious grin making everything else fade into oblivion. Memories from a life that now feels like an ethereal dream flicker rapidly through my mind: skipping school to dash off to the lake, collapsing into fits of laughter by its tranquil edge.

I blink against a biting gust of wind, my cheeks stinging from both the cold and these resurfacing memories. Brayden's teasing voice seems to follow me around every corner, warm and inviting yet just out of reach in the present moment.

My heart clenches in my chest as I wander aimlessly, the weight of my emotions threatening to shatter the fragile calm I'm desperately clinging onto. Memories of the heart break that sent me fleeing to New York City flood back, mingling with the silent worry in my mother's eyes for my father that eventually drew me back. It all feels too close for comfort; past and present colliding like winter melting into spring. Doubts creep in, making me wonder if this town will ever allow me to move forward, or if I'll ever be ready to take that step.

The air bites at my skin with its icy grip, but despite its chill, warm memories seep into each step I take, lending a shaky determination to my stride. My breath fogs up before me, disappearing almost as quickly as it forms while I draw closer to the familiar silhouette of the treehouse standing tall in the farm field. Its sturdy and obstinate presence is a stark reminder of Brayden - the boy who once held my heart so tightly.

An invisible force draws me towards it, making it feel like all those years away were nothing more than fleeting moments. My gaze sweeps over the treehouse before settling on the softly glowing Grace Hollow Church near-by. A lone figure moves within it, arranging chairs for tomorrow's service - an act that strikes me as both odd and beautiful at once.

I let my eyes drift back to our old refuge where shad-ows of our past linger – hours spent cocooned in dreams of forever and promises that now seem simultaneously within reach and light years away. The wind picks up its pace, shaking the wooden structure and causing tremors in my heart. But there I stand; still amidst it all as moon-light bathes me in a gentle glow of hope that refuses to dim out.

I stand frozen in the shadow of the treehouse, its wood-en skeleton towering above me like a silent guardian of long-held secrets. It remains weathered and untouched by time, each splinter and knot a tangible echo of who Brayden and I used to be, of dreams we once dared to weave together. My breath hangs heavy in the cold air as I let my mind wander back to nights spent nestled within its timeworn walls, his voice whispering promises that felt as unbreakable as they were tender. A gust of wind toys with a loose strand of my hair, drawing it across my eyes, and I brush it away with a hand that trembles just enough to betray my composure. So deeply am I entrenched in these echoes from our past that the sudden roar of an approaching car startles me, yanking me harshly back into the present. I whirl around, feeling every bit like a ghost from my own history ensnared in the merciless glare of oncoming headlights.

The figure stepping out of the vehicle is a Sheriff officer. The crunch of his boots on frost-coated grass echoes in the quiet night as he approaches. "Tess," he announces, his voice a ghost from my past, lingering heavy in the chilly air—Carl Johnson.

I don't shy away or avoid his gaze but meet it head-on with a spark of the old defiance that still burns within me. It's him who breaks our silent standoff first, perhaps impressed by my resilience or maybe just eager to dispel the awkwardness of our reunion. As he steps further into the cold, his breath transforms into swirling mists around his head in the frigid air.

"Didn't think I'd run into you here," he says, his voice deep and laden with the resonance of our intertwined history. Our eyes meet, and I'm momentarily ensnared in that same fierce determination that had driven me to flee all those years ago. A hint of a smile almost graces his face, but it quickly gives way to a cautious neutrality. He's holding back, just like me - both of us careful not to bare too much too soon.

The first words between us hang awkwardly in the icy air, stunted and laden with a past we've both been carrying. "Carl," I manage to say, my voice battling against the biting cold.

My jaw clenches instinctively, as if preparing for an incoming blow. He studies me intently, taking note of my defensive posture - like a fighter anticipating the next hit. The scandal has left its mark on me, that much is clear to him, but it hasn't crushed my spirit. He's seen many fold under less pressure. That's probably why he doesn't pull any punches.

"I bet you didn't think you'd see me either," he quips, a hint of dry wit lacing his words. "Still around after all this time. Someone's got to keep the peace."

I press my lips into a tight line, defiance and resignation battling for dominance on my face. "Things don't seem to change much in this town, do they?" I retort, old hurts seeping into my tone.

He nods slowly, as if absorbing the weight of my words. "You might be surprised," he responds, eyes never leaving mine.

I brace myself for the question I know is on its way. "You heard about Brayden?" he asks, his voice soft yet straightforward.

An involuntary flicker of emotion crosses my face before I manage to regain control.

"Pastor Brayden," he continues, a slight crack in his typically gruff exterior. "I'll admit, I didn't see it coming."

I swallow hard, the tension manifesting as I hold my breath. For a moment, Carl seems to soften with something akin to sympathy. Maybe he'd always known I wasn't as guilty as the town believed. Maybe that's why he speaks again.

"Back then," he begins, his eyes fixed on mine with an intensity that makes me squirm a little, "things weren't exactly what they seemed. You remember I was just a deputy then."

His words hang in the chilly night air between us, heavy with unspoken truths.

I'm taken aback, my mind racing to piece together what he's implying, but I keep my face neutral. Instead of responding immediately, I fold my arms tightly across my chest, both to ward off the biting cold and to shield myself from the weight of his revelation. What's he getting at?

"I guess not everyone thought so," I say, my voice a shaky mix of bitterness and relief.

Carl just shrugs, a gesture that feels like an unspoken apology. "Folks around here... they prefer their stories simple," he replies, rubbing his hands together to chase away the chill.

I catch him noticing the flicker in my eyes, one that's now mingled with uncertainty. I'm not sure if I can trust what he's offering.

The conversation shifts awkwardly, more out of necessity than comfort. "Your folks doing all right?" Carl asks, his gruff tone softening slightly.

I nod, pausing before speaking. "They're the same as ever," I admit. "They were determined to have me home for Christmas." There's so much unsaid in my words—the pressure of expectations, the hope for mending old wounds.

Carl studies me closely, seeing the runaway girl and the woman I've become, both eager to know if there's still a place for me here.

"Well," Carl finally says, stretching the word like he's testing its weight. "I'm sure they're glad to have you back." He gives me a nod—a quiet gesture of peace and understanding.

I watch him head back to his patrol car, the engine grumbling to life and shattering the night's silence. I stand there, rooted in place, feeling the impact of our brief exchange linger as his taillights fade into the distance. The chill deepens without the engine's hum, wrapping around me like a cloak of solitude and anticipation. My gaze drifts back to the treehouse before landing on the softly glowing church. Inside, a lone figure shifts about, stacking hymnals and stirring memories long tucked away. My breath puffs out in small clouds as I turn towards home, thoughts swirling around Brayden, our past, and what tomorrow might bring. I'm not sure what to do.

Three

M y mother's deft fingers mix the cookie dough as if it were second nature, while mine fumble awkwardly beside her. She measures flour without need of a measuring cup and cracks eggs with precision I can only admire.

"So, how's life in New York?" she asks, her voice gently probing for more than a simple answer.

"Busy," I reply, forcing a smile that doesn't quite reach my eyes.

My clumsy attempts to measure out the dough into precise cookie size result in it sticking stubbornly to my fingers. The rich aroma of butter and sugar envelops us, and I can't help but feel a pang of regret for not having spent more time like this growing up. It feels strangely comforting being here together, yet my gaze keeps drifting towards the window, betraying my unease.

Outside the window, the world is cold and white, but inside, the kitchen is a sanctuary of warmth and cluttered familiarity.

The curtains above the sink are new to me—bright with a cheerful Christmas pattern I don't recognize. It's not surprising, considering how many years it's been since I've been home, and knowing Mom, she's likely updated her holiday decor again, weaving fresh warmth into the kitchen each year.

My mother wears a red apron that I do recognize from years ago, a little frayed but still serving its purpose, and I can almost pretend the years apart were a brief, inconsequential dream. I find myself remembering the way she used to let me lick the batter when I was small.

"Haven't seen much of that busy life," she says, glancing at me with a smile that tries to reach beyond my answer.

I shrug, looking at my fingers as they attempt to ball sticky dough. "You know how it is."

The words feel hollow, and I know she can hear it in my voice. Her smile softens with understanding, or maybe it's patience, as if she expects the truth to spill out eventually. I scrape the flour from the counter with my hand, trying to gather my thoughts along with it.

The smell of baking cookies fills the room, rich and sweet, and it pulls me back into memories I thought I'd left behind. Memories of a house full of laughter and light, of snowy afternoons spent in this very kitchen before everything changed. I watch my mother as she wipes her hands on her apron and wonders aloud about Brayden, asking if I've seen him yet. Her voice carries a tone of innocent curiosity, but it stabs at old wounds, and I don't trust myself to respond.

We move to the table, and I pick up the rolling pin, fumbling with the weight of it. Its wooden surface is worn smooth from years of use, but it feels awkward in my hands. We roll out the dough for a batch of sugar cookies, or rather, my mother rolls while I try to keep up, and she guides the cookie cutters with years of expertise. I press them in haphazardly, and the soft clink of metal against the countertop echoes my uncertainty. It's strange how naturally she works around my stumbles, as if expecting me to be lost in a place I never quite found.

I pause for a moment, watching her carefully fix each piece of my mangled attempts at cookie cutting, before speaking. "I should have come home sooner," I say, surprising myself with the honesty of my words.

Her hands still for just a moment, and I hear the intake of breath before she answers. "All things in their own time," she says gently. Her fingers move again, sure and deliberate, and I can see the relief in her face even as she tries to keep her tone light.

I nod, feeling a strange mix of comfort and guilt. The words I want to say stay tangled in my throat. I'm here now, I think, but is it too late? The cookies line the trays, ready for the oven, and the sight of them fills me with a sudden, aching nostalgia. All those years I convinced myself I was too busy, too caught up in my own life to be part of this one. And here I am, back in the place I ran from, back with the people I left behind. The cookies bake, and the scent wraps around me like a warm, persistent memory.

The kitchen feels smaller than I remember, more crowded with the ghosts of the past than with the stacks of old cookbooks and flour-dusted countertops. Christmas music plays softly from the living room, and the sounds blend into the background like the faded wallpaper.

I glance up and see her watching me, a look of cautious hope in her eyes. "I'm glad you came back, Tess," she says, the words simple but full of unspoken layers.

I nod, swallowing hard against the swell of emotion. "Me too," I manage, though the truth of it scares me.

We pull the trays from the oven, and the cookies sit in neat rows, golden and perfect. My mother moves with her usual grace, as if this moment is no different from all the others, as if the years apart were just a long pause between baking days. I let myself enjoy it, the two of us here, working together in the kitchen like no time has passed. And for a brief moment, I almost believe it.

Then a knock at the door shatters the spell, sudden and polite. My hands freeze, and I see my mother's expression shift from serene to questioning.

"Who could that be?" she muses, her curiosity unguarded. "I'll get it," I say, though I feel a reluctance to leave the warmth of the kitchen.

My steps are slow, the familiar creak of the floorboards beneath me a reminder of the home I've missed, the home I fled. My fingers hesitate on the cold doorknob, a sudden rush of doubt making me pause. I take a breath and pull it open.

A rush of winter air accompanies the cheerful face that greets me. "Hi, Tess!" Hannah Spencer stands at the threshold, her smile bright and warm enough to rival the heat of the oven.

Her dark hair spills out from under a knitted hat, and she looks every bit the girl I remember, only grown now, more assured and impossibly kind.

"Wow, Hannah," I say, taken aback by the ease of her welcome. "It's been a long time."

Her presence catches me off guard, dragging memories of better days behind it, days when the world felt safe and my future wasn't yet shaped by leaving.

"It has," she agrees with a nod, her breath visible in the chilly air. "I almost didn't recognize you with that city-girl look!"

Her teasing is gentle, a reminder of the playful camaraderie we used to share when I used to do it to her when she was just a little kid following me around. I find myself smiling despite the awkwardness I feel.

My mother appears beside me, her surprise quickly melting into pleasure. "Hannah! Look at you," she exclaims, drawing her into a quick, affectionate hug. "What brings you out in this cold?"

Hannah's eyes twinkle, and I see her gaze shift between us, taking in the scene she has interrupted. "I came with a mission," she says, holding up her gloved hands in mock seriousness. "Brayden asked me to extend his invitation for you to help with our Christmas pageant."

The words hang in the air, carrying a quiet weight I can't shake. For years, I've tried not to think of him—pushed his name and the memories it carried into a locked corner of my mind. But now that I'm home, his name keeps surfacing, quietly threading its way into conversations, tugging at memories I've fought to keep buried. *Brayden.* Saying it aloud feels strange, as if it's testing the walls I've built, letting the past rush in when I least expect it.

Hannah watches my reaction, her expression softening as she sees the conflict she has stirred. "You don't have to decide right away," she adds quickly, sensing the turmoil beneath my stillness. "Just think about it, okay?"

I nod, unable to find words that won't betray the emotions rolling around inside me. The safety of the kitchen feels miles away, and I stand there, caught between the comforting moment I'm having with my mother and the complicated past that awaits beyond the door.

"Thank you, Hannah," my mother says, filling the silence with her usual grace. "Tell Brayden we'll work on convincing her."

Hannah laughs, a light, musical sound that I didn't realize I missed until this moment. "I'll do that," she promises. Her eyes meet mine again, earnest and full of an understanding I don't deserve. "It's really good to see you, Tess. I hope you'll come." The cold air rushes in again as she waves and turns to leave, her footprints soft and new in the snow. I watch her go, a part of me wanting to call her back, another part wanting to shut the door on everything she's brought with her. My hand lingers on the knob, my heart heavy with the choice I know I'll have to make. I close the door and turn back to my mother, who stands waiting with the kind of patience only she can muster.

"What do you think?" she asks, her voice gentle, devoid of pressure but full of a mother's knowing.

I swallow hard, feeling the distance between the years and now collapse around me. "I think," I say slowly, each word carefully placed, "it's a lot to take in." My voice trembles just a little, and the crack is enough to release a flood of everything I've kept locked away.

We return to the kitchen, but the simplicity of the moment has shifted, replaced by the quiet weight of things left unsaid. The warm scent of cookies still hangs in the air, mingling with the unspoken questions between us. We sit at the table, the ease from before already slipping away. I glance at my mother, at the gentle certainty in her eyes, and find myself wishing I could borrow even a fraction of that quiet faith.

"Brayden must really want you to be there," she says softly, breaking a half-cooled cookie in half and offering me a gooey piece. I take it, a strange mix of warmth and unease settling in my chest.

I shrug, but I can't quite keep the flicker of hope from showing. "Maybe." The word hangs between us, full of possibilities and fears, and I feel the weight of them all pressing down, a tangled mix of past and present that only I can sort through.

I meet her eyes and nod, even though I've still not made up my mind. "Maybe I'll go."

The thought terrifies me, but it also ignites a spark of some- thing I haven't felt in years. The beginnings of courage, perhaps, or the first step toward something like forgiveness. My mother smiles, and I think she sees the spark too. *What do I do?*

Four

The bell above the diner's door jingles softly as I step inside, drawing a quiet glance from the morning crowd. The air is warm and heavy with the comforting scent of frying bacon and eggs, mingled with the rich aroma of fresh coffee and buttered toast. Somewhere behind the counter, the steady hiss of the griddle and the clatter of silverware create a familiar, rhythmic soundtrack. The walls glow with red and green—garlands draped along windows, wreaths hung with care—and a Santa figurine smiles knowingly from the counter, part of the diner's quiet holiday charm. I pause in the doorway, caught between the hum of conversation and the hush of curious stares, as the warmth of the room settles around me.

I slide my hands into my coat pockets and weave through the maze of tables where plaid shirts and woolen scarves crowd around steaming mugs of coffee. People talk over their breakfasts in low murmurs—quiet enough to keep their words hidden, but not enough to hide the fact they're talking about me. The Maple Ridge Diner hums with the soft buzz of conversation, carrying a current of curiosity that settles around me like a weight.

Mabel spots me first, waving from a booth with a smile that could warm a blizzard. Her silver hair catches the light like a halo, and she's wearing a red cardigan dotted with snowmen. I've known her my whole life—long enough to feel safe in her presence, long enough to worry about what she'll say about me returning to the church I thought I left behind forever. She's been like family, watching over me since I was a kid, and the years haven't dulled her ability to see right through me. I'm not surprised she was the first to reach out, inviting me here with one of her famous "just to catch up" notes. I can't help but grin back as I head over.

"Theresa," she says, her voice wrapping around the name like a warm hug.

"Mabel," I reply, shrugging out of my coat. I slide into the seat across from her, and she nudges a steaming mug of coffee in my direction.

"I took the liberty," she says with a twinkle in her eye. "How do you take it?"

I nod, grateful. "Oh...just black."

The clatter of plates and the murmur of morning chatter swirl around us. I take a sip of coffee, letting the warmth spread through me, wishing it could melt away the knot in my stomach. "The place looks... festive," I say, glancing around at the overdone decorations.

Mabel chuckles, adjusting the snowflake pin on her cardigan. "Every year, Earl adds more lights. I'm convinced he's trying to signal Santa from space."

I laugh, and it feels good—like stretching my legs after a long night studying. But it fades quickly as I set the mug down and fold my hands in my lap. Hannah's invitation burns in my mind, the harder I try to stamp it down.

"I got an invitation," I start, my voice shaky as I fidget with the corner of the napkin. "An invitation to the Christmas pageant."

Mabel watches me, her eyes kind and knowing. "The church still remembers your costumes. They'd love to see you there." "I don't know if I belong there anymore," I admit, my words heavy with years of doubt and distance.

Mabel's weathered hands wrap around her mug, and she waits a moment before speaking. "Time and distance don't change everything, dear. Sometimes they just help us see things more clearly."

I pick at the napkin until it looks as torn as I feel. "I wish it was that simple. Coming back... it's like I've been gone a hundred years. Like I'm some stranger."

She leans forward, her gaze gentle but steady. "It's only been 13 years, Tess. And you're not a stranger to everyone."

I sigh, staring into my coffee. It mirrors the chaos of my mind—swirling, unsettled. "I didn't exactly leave on the best terms."

Mabel reaches across the table, her touch as light as a whisper. "People understand more than you think. You've carried the blame for too long."

The diner's Christmas music hums softly, weaving through the air like a tender reminder of the season. I struggle to hold Mabel's gaze, feeling exposed, my old defenses crumbling like gingerbread. "What if nothing's changed, Mabel? What if everything's just... waiting for me to mess up again?"

"The Bible says to 'forgive each other if you have a grievance against someone.' But it also says to 'Forgive as the Lord forgave you.' Sometimes though...the hardest person to forgive is yourself," she says, her voice so gentle it nearly breaks me.

I bite my lip, holding back the tide of emotions that threaten to spill over. The quiet between us feels heavy, carrying the weight of our conversation. I nod slowly, absorbing her words, feeling the tiniest glimmer of something I haven't felt in years—hope.

Mabel's words wrap around me like a soft scarf, but across the diner, I see a set of eyes paying way too much attention to me. The blonde woman hides behind a newspaper, though not well enough to fool anyone. The morning light glints off the giant rock on her finger and the knowing glint in her eye. Even from here, I feel the sting of her curiosity, so sharp and precise that it should come with a surgeon's license. She lowers her paper just enough for a slow, insincere smile that sours in the air between us.

It's Nancy Miller. Her smile may be sweet, but I know her well enough to taste the judgment underneath. My shoulders tighten, the old fear creeping back in. I wrap my hands around the coffee mug to stop their shaking, trying to focus on Mabel's comforting presence across the table.

"You look like you're carrying the world on those shoulders," Mabel says gently, watching me with patient eyes. I attempt a shrug, but it feels like a lie.

"It's just...I feel like everyone is watching me," I tell her, my voice barely above a whisper. The clink of silverware and the low hum of conversation feel louder; all directed at me.

Mabel's gaze never wavers, a rock against the tide of my insecurities. "People will always talk, Tess," she says, reaching for my hand. "That doesn't mean you have to listen."

I sigh, feeling the weight of the diner's eyes and my own doubt. Nancy shifts in her seat, her paper rustling like it's alive with rumors. Her very presence makes the air crackle with expectation, and I can't help but shrink beneath it. I glance over and catch her peeking again, leaning toward us like she's tuning into a soap opera.

"I feel like everyone thinks they know what happened," I say, pulling my hand back and wrapping it around my mug again.

"They're just waiting for me to confirm it."

Mabel leans closer, her warmth a barrier against the cold whispers I imagine swirling around us. "You've carried this burden alone for too long," she tells me, her voice like a balm on an old wound. "Maybe it's time to talk about it with others."

Nancy drops her paper just long enough to check her watch. It's an exaggerated move, as if to remind me how my time here is running out. I fight the urge to duck my head like a scolded child.

Mabel's hand is on mine again, steady and unyielding. "Give yourself a chance to find peace," Mabel says, her tone a gentle nudge in the right direction. "Trust yourself, Tess. Trust the people who care about you. And...dare I say? Trust The Lord."

The clatter and chatter swell around us, the sound of a dozen breakfasts eaten by a dozen curious ears. I watch Nancy gather her things, slow and deliberate. She pauses on her way out, an unnecessary linger near our table that speaks volumes. Her smile is bright, her eyes brighter, full of things unsaid and ready to be spread. I just want to stick my tongue out at her.

I grip my coffee cup, feeling the slight tremor in my hands. Nancy walks past, and the tension follows her out, leaving me raw and exposed. Mabel squeezes my hand, anchoring me back to our conversation. Back to her unwavering belief in me.

"You're stronger than you think," she says, eyes filled with kindness. "I mean...you're a doctor."

My resolve wavers, the old doubts battling with the new hope she's trying to plant. "What if I go back, and nothing's changed? What if I haven't changed enough?"

"Change starts in the heart, dear," Mabel replies with a knowing smile. "Yours is already in the right place."

I nod, not trusting myself to speak without betraying the emotions threatening to spill over. The diner is still busy, still buzzing, but without Nancy's piercing presence, it feels less overwhelming. Mabel watches me carefully, waiting for me to find my footing.

I take a long sip of coffee, letting its warmth bolster the flicker of determination Mabel's trying to light within me. It's fragile, but it's there, and as I set the mug down, I allow myself to feel the tiniest bit reassured. The town's judgment might still loom, but for the first time, I'm not sure it matters as much as I thought.

Mabel waits with the patience of a saint. Her quiet understanding is almost too much, and I stare into my coffee, pretending to find answers there. The breakfast crowd thins around us, leaving the diner as bare as my own options. A waitress breezes by with a pot of coffee, her apron jingling like an unkept promise. I close my eyes and let the scents and sounds of Christmas swallow me whole.

The garlands seem less cheerful with each passing minute, the twinkling lights blinking away the last of my resolve. I take a deep breath, and the room feels thick with quiet tension. I can't tell if it's Christmas or my own memories that are making it hard to breathe.

The waitress stops at our table, filling our cups with a smile that lingers in the steam. Mabel thanks her and waits for me to speak, her silence more understanding than anything I deserve. "Why would he even want me involved?" I finally ask, my voice as fragile as I feel. I look up, and the earnest concern in Mabel's eyes nearly undoes me. "As far as he knows...what if I don't even celebrate Christmas anymore?" I add, the words falling between us like snowflakes on a dark coat, melting before they leave a mark.

"We both know that's not true, dear," Mabel replies softly. "And Christmas reminds us that miracles happen in the most unexpected places."

I shake my head, my skepticism like a stone in my chest. The diner seems emptier by the minute, and with it, my ability to hide from Mabel's gaze.

"What if I don't fit in?" I say, a tremor in my voice. "What if I don't belong here anymore?"

"You belonged here long before you ever left," Mabel assures me, her smile so full of warmth it stings. "Give Pastor Braydon— and yourself—a chance."

I stare into the fresh cup of coffee, the dark liquid like a miniature storm, reflecting the chaos in my heart. "You make it sound so easy."

Mabel laughs, a soft, melodic sound. "Maybe because I've seen it happen so many times before."

The diner's holiday cheer seems overwhelming now, a bright contrast to the uncertainty I can't shake. The clock on the wall ticks like a countdown, marking each moment of hesitation. I close my eyes, feeling time and the season slip through my fingers.

"I wish I could believe, like you do," I admit, my hands cradling the warmth of the mug as if it could offer me some comfort.

Mabel watches me, her silence filled with faith. I want to soak it in; let it fill the places I've left empty for too long.

"Why did you come back?" Mabel asks, her voice gentle, curious.

"Because my dad..." I started.

"No...that's the excuse," she interrupted. "What's the real reason you came back?"

I pause for a moment to consider her words. "Because I couldn't stay away any longer," I confess. "I couldn't keep running."

"Then you've already changed more than you know," Mabel says, beaming at me as if I'm the one handing out Christmas miracles.

I weigh her words, feeling the smallest flicker of determination rise within me. It gives me a quiet sense that something good might still be possible. I take a deep breath and let that thought settle inside me.

"I'll do it," I say, the conviction in my voice surprising us both. "I'll help with the pageant. Maybe it's time I stopped running."

Mabel's eyes shine, the approval in them warming me from the inside out. I feel something open up in my chest, a lightness I haven't felt since I left Maple Ridge all those years ago.

The decision wraps around me, and with it, a newfound resolve. My posture straightens, my shoulders lifting like a weight has fallen away. My eyes meet Mabel's, clearer than they've been since I arrived.

"Miracles really do happen," she says with a mischievous glint in her eye, just as I'm mid-swallow. Coffee burns up my nose, and I cough through a startled laugh. Mabel bursts into laughter, the sound carrying across the diner and filling it with unexpected joy.

Silverware clinks against plates and murmured conversations blend into a soothing hum as we slide from the booth. I button my coat with steadier hands than before, stealing glances at Mabel who tucks her scarf just so, the way she's probably done every winter for decades. Her weathered fingers pat my arm as we turn toward the door, and something in the gesture anchors me against the fear waiting beyond the frosted windows.

The diner's bell jingles above us as we leave, and for the first time, it sounds like hope.

Five

I stand at the bottom of the steps, staring up at the church doors like they're holding their breath—just like me. My palms are damp, and I can't decide if it's the heat of my gloves or my nerves. Probably both.

I don't know what I'm walking into. Faces frozen in time, expectations I can't meet, whispered questions I'm not ready to answer. But more than anyone else...it's Brayden.

Pastor Brayden, now.

The title echoes in my head, sharp and strange. He's the reason I can't breathe right. The reason my stomach is twisted in knots as I reach for the door. I wonder what he'll say—if he'll say anything at all. Maybe he won't even look at me. Maybe he'll smile that careful, polished smile he saves for strangers and pretend our history never happened.

I press my hand to the door. For a second, I think about turning around. But Hannah was nice enough to personally invite me, and I'm tired of running from the past. And whatever's waiting inside—I need to face it.

The church smells of polished wood and warm coffee, with a faint hint of pine from the seasonal decorations. The deep burgundy carpet I remember is gone, replaced with a softer, neutral tone that looks fresh underfoot. Christmas music drifts in from behind the sanctuary's closed doors. I try to hold my head high, but it's a losing battle. I keep seeing us here as teenagers, the brink of adulthood blurred by midnight carols and secrets stashed behind the choir loft. I keep seeing him.

Hannah's voice floats from the side room, bright as a bell. "Tess! You made it!" She's in her element, juggling a phone, a clipboard, and a tower of plastic costume bins, barely breaking her stride as she breezes toward me. "Come in, come in! You want coffee or cider? We've got both, and if you say neither I'll assume you've been taken over by aliens."

I almost laugh, a real one. "Coffee, if there's any left." "Always for you," she chirps, already darting to the kitchenette to pour a cup. Her energy is contagious—the nerves in my stomach settle by a degree.

Once she returned with the steaming drink, I follow her into the sanctuary past a nativity set so elaborate it could only have been masterminded by someone a touch obsessive. (Almost certainly Mabel, who once hand-painted gold leaf halos on every angel). I remem-

ber one Christmas years ago, a lively argument breaking out over when Baby Jesus should be placed in the
manger. Some insisted it should wait until Christmas Eve,
while others—like my family—wanted him there with the
completed display. Even now, seeing the scene set a full
week before Christmas brings that memory rushing back,
warm and stubborn as ever.

The gathering is smaller than I expect – just a handful of
people, heads ducked over paper programs and spread-
sheets, already circled up on the church's front stage. I
see instantly that nothing has changed and everything
has: Mabel sitting on the front pew, acting as adminis-
trator; Mrs. Keane, the forever Sunday

School teacher, meticulously labeling boxes of sheep
ears and cardboard wings; a pre-teen boy with the unmistakable posture of open rebellion hunched over a
stack of scripts. The men— one in a neon hunting cap,
one with a beard that could shelter a family of wrens—are
wrangling a tangle of extension cords like it's an Olympic
sport. The scene hums with the old rhythm, as if my
absence never registered in the DNA of the place.

Hannah, radiating logistics, flits away to place a calm-
ing hand on the script boy, murmuring something that
makes him blush. I hover at the edge, debating whether
to sit—where, how, with whom?—but Mabel stands, arms
outstretched in greeting. She hugs me as if she hasn't
already saved my day once this week. For an instant, the

scent of her lavender lotion and the soft wool of her sweater make me a kid again, unafraid. Then she lets me go, and I'm back to the present, slightly adrift. I glance down at my cup, brushing a stray drop of coffee from my sleeve with a faint smile.

"You came!" she beams, squeezing my arm in both hands. "Pastor will be pleased. He's been hoping you'd…" she stops, reading my face, and pivots smoothly. "He'll be glad you can help. The angel costumes are in catastrophe."

Pastor Brayden. I glance at the bins and try to will my pulse to slow. "Catastrophe's putting it gently," I say, and Mabel gives me a conspiratorial wink before moving off to break up a squabble over which donkey gets to stand closest to baby Jesus this year (apparently, there's a hierarchy).

I go to my knees beside the costume bins, using the familiar task as a shield. My fingers find wire and fabric wings, glue-glittered halos, several beards that smell faintly of old coffee and new stress. It steadies me, a little, sorting disaster into order. The bins are labeled but wrong, the contents jumbled and—just as

I'm telling myself that's the worst of it—I see a pair of shoes pause in my peripheral vision. Brown cowboy boots, well-worn. My heart takes off at a gallop.

"Need a hand?"

The voice is the same as I remember, but deeper, steadier. Not the reckless boy who talked me into midnight hikes along the ridge, but something new— a calm I almost resent.

He lowers himself to a crouch, jeans and flannel shirt crisp and clean, making eye contact. Brayden James. The name alone has its own gravitational pull. He looks the same, only different. The sandy brown hair is familiar, but now there's a short beard that surprises me—suits him, in fact. Some of the edge has been sanded down, but there's a glint behind his caring blue eyes that says he remembers, too.

"Hi, Pastor Brayden." My voice comes out small but even, which is the best I can hope for.

He gives a crooked half-smile, the kind that once meant trouble or a dare. "Hey, Tess." He gestures at the wings, then at the mounting disaster of the pageant prep. "Still know your way around a hot glue gun?"

"I could probably fix these with my eyes closed," I say before I can stop myself.

His laugh is soft, and it does something to my pulse I wish it wouldn't. "Some things never change." His tone is warm but careful, like he's handling something fragile, and I realize it might be me. He reaches for a halo missing half its glitter, spins it in his hand. "We tried to fill your shoes," he says, "but, turns out, no one's got your particular brand of Christmas pageant magic."

His words should embarrass me, but instead they settle somewhere deep, winding around the place in my chest that's felt empty for too long. I look at him—really look—and for a moment, all the miles and years and what-ifs collapse. We're just two people on the floor of the same church we grew up in, surrounded by the same mess, pretending that we haven't been apart for years.

He twirls the gold pipe cleaner around his finger, and for a heartbeat I am flung back to our first pageant together—third grade Mary and Joseph, him nearly fainting when he had to hold my hand on stage while the whole congregation watched. It takes everything I have not to stare too long now.

He glances over at me, and now the smile is softer, tired at the edges but real. "Wasn't sure you'd show."

"I almost didn't," I admit, fishing a wrinkled angel robe from the bin. "But, apparently, this place has a gravitational pull."

He mumbles his agreement. "That's for sure."

I laugh before I can dissect whether it's safe to. "Pastor, huh?" "Doctor, huh?" He shows me a glimpse of that mischievous smile I fondly remember.

I groan and shake my head. "Please don't remind me. I'm just Tess here, okay?"

"Deal," he says, lips quirking. "But only if you call me Brayden. Not 'Pastor.' Makes me sound even older than I am." His voice is lighter now, but there's a layer underneath, something like relief or gratitude. I'm not sure I want to dig deeper just yet.

He starts to say something else, but Mrs. Keane snaps her fingers from across the room. "Pastor Brayden! If you could please not distract our best hope at fixing these wings, I might actually get these sheep organized before rehearsal starts." She gives him a look—strict but not unkind—and he holds up both hands in mock surrender. His eyes linger a heartbeat extra on me before he stands, brushing imaginary dust off his jeans.

"Nice seeing you again, Tess," he says, voice lower. "Let me know if you need help." I smile, though I'm sure it comes out half-heartedly.

Volunteer coordination turns out to be half costuming and half referee. By the time the fourth glue gun comes out (whose idea was it to have four, anyway?), I'm covered in glitter and rogue strands of hot glue, and everyone's arguing about whether the Magi should wear crowns or turbans this year. The mothers in charge of shepherds have staged a miniature mutiny on the front pew, demanding equal pizazz for their kids' costumes, and the Wise Men's parents are lobbying for actual gold spray-paint, which instantly becomes a fire hazard in everyone's imagination.

The evening swirls by, one disaster after another, but the rhythm of sorting and fixing settles into something like fun. When the angel costumes have their halos restored, I'm handed a roll of duct tape and given the task of "repairing" the sagging stable when no one else can agree on a plan. It feels good to use my hands, to make sense of the chaos all around me, to hear laughter ring through the church where I once knew every creaking floorboard.

Even the noise starts to seem familiar, like a song I used to know. I'm surprised by how much I've missed it—how, without realizing it, I find myself softly singing along to Go Tell It on the Mountain drifting from the small speaker on the stage. I recognize the song, though the artist—MercyMe—doesn't ring a bell. The words slip out anyway, as if they've been tucked somewhere in my memory all along. How much I've missed having a place, even a small one, in the commotion.

We finally clear the last of the mess, and the oldest Wise Man holds the door as parents bustle kids into the snow-covered evening. "See you tomorrow!" Mrs. Keane calls, and I realize with a start she means me.

"Same time, same place," Mabel echoes, giving my shoulder a squeeze. "This pageant might come together yet!"

Her words echo as I linger in the quiet, gathering my coat. I catch sight of a forgotten shepherd's staff, glue-gunned gold and leaning haphazardly against the altar, and I leave it there like a promise.

The parking lot is emptying fast. The air is crisp and the stars peek out from a sky as deep and dark as my childhood memories. I think about the light and warmth inside, the bustle of people who may still remember me as the girl who left without saying goodbye. Maybe, I tell myself as I unlock my car, I don't have to stay that girl. Maybe I can put the past behind me.

I'm still turning it over in my mind when a voice calls my name across the snow. Brayden stands by his truck, hands tucked into his pockets, breath misting in the cold. "Need a ride?" he asks, and the way he says it almost sounds like old times.

"I've got it," I call back, but I can't keep the smile—unexpected, tentative, but mine—from my voice. "See you, Brayden." I say his name like I say it every day.

He waves, and in this light, with that beard, he looks... interesting. There's something about him that catches me. *Nope. It's just a beard. Just a voice. Just him saying goodnight. Nothing more.* I tell myself there's nothing there—though the slight tug of curiosity in my chest disagrees.

Six

At breakfast, the pancakes are fluffy and the conversation thick enough to choke on.

Dad's already at the table, shirt pressed and coffee mug parked at twelve o'clock, exact as always. Mom stands at the stove, spatula tapping a twitchy pattern on the skillet while the music, from the living room, hums Wham!'s "Last Christmas" over the hiss and pop of bacon. I try to slip into my seat unnoticed, but Mom clocks me with a glance that runs from my bedhead down to the lint on my hoodie. Dad doesn't even bother with the courtesy scan, just lifts his chin and waits.

I'm not sure whether he expects me to confess or explain, and so I just mumble, "Morning," and hope that's enough.

Mom slides a stack of pancakes onto my plate, the top one crowned by an accidental smiley face of melting butter. Crispy strips of bacon sizzle on the side, filling the air with their savory aroma. She glances toward the door with a small, amused smile. "And you didn't need to lock every lock," she says softly, her tone laced with gentle humor. "You know you don't need to, here, right? It's Maple Ridge, not New York."

"Sorry, Mom," I say, though it comes out automatic and lazy, like muscle memory.

I scroll through my phone under the table, pretending to check the weather, though I'm mostly avoiding the quiet between us. Dad stirs his coffee slowly, his gaze drifting toward the window. There's no real intensity in him—just the easy stillness of someone used to mornings like this—but it only makes my own awkwardness feel sharper.

"Your mother tells me you're helping out at the church again," he says at last, his voice carrying a quiet warmth that catches me off guard.

I wince and wait out the silence, hoping it will dissolve on its own. But nothing about Dad is self-solving. I already know the next words will have a point.

"It's just the Christmas pageant," I say, picking at the smiley butter until it's a messy frown. "Hannah asked. It's not some big…" I trail off, catching the way he's looking at me. It's not disappointment I see—just something I can't quite place. In my mind, it feels like he's quietly measuring me, weighing what I've done and what I haven't, as if trying to decide whether I'm still the same girl he once knew. *I feel like a kid again.*

The explanation sounds thin even to my own ears; I brace myself, expecting him to launch into a lecture. He nods, and the pause stretches long enough that I almost relax—until he speaks, direct and unflinching. "It's good you're finding ways to... reconnect. With the community. And with the Lord." I look up, caught off guard. I'd been bracing for a reprimand, not a compliment.

Mom sits, smoothing her napkin over her robe. She's watching me, too, her dark eyes soft and searching. "We're just glad you're back, honey. Even for a little while." She pats my hand, a tiny squeeze that almost gets me choked up. "I know it's not easy."

I want to laugh, but I don't trust the sound that would come out. "It's just a Christmas play, Mom. I'm not up for sainthood."

"Everyone has to start somewhere," Dad says, deadpan, but I catch the flicker of a smile before he hides it in his coffee.

I stare at the pancakes, the mess of syrup making sticky rivers between the islands of half-melted butter and uneaten bacon. A commercial breaks up the music and suddenly Mom is talking about the neighbor's cat getting stuck in their dryer vent, and I ride out the reprieve in silence.

But Dad's not done. He clears his throat with the kind of finality that means business. "Your mother says you might be home longer than planned."

This isn't a question. Not really. More a gentle shove toward the subject we've all circled but no one's wanted to land on.

I push the pancakes around, reluctant. "It depends on your health...you haven't told me what's wrong. And I told the ER they can manage for a few weeks without me." I stop there, but Dad doesn't flinch at the word "ER" or follow the bait about a health scare. He's too stubborn for that. He'd ignore a heart attack as long as he could drive himself to the hospital.

Mom catches my eye over the table, her gaze tender but braced for impact. "We want you to stay as long as you need. As long as you want, Theresa."

I nod, and for a brief moment, I feel the soft landing of belonging—then Dad sets his mug down with a careful thud.

"We know why you left," he says, the words so gentle they barely leave a mark. "But it doesn't mean you have to keep punishing yourself." He says it with the same conviction he used to recite scripture at the dinner table, back when I believed prayer would solve all of our problems.

I blink, startled, and look up. "I'm not..." I start, but Dad's already shaking his head, a little smile pulling at the corner of his mouth.

"You are. You always have."

He's not wrong. I always have. Every test, every shift, every sleepless night at the hospital—punishment, penance, pick your word. I look at him, really look, and realize he's just letting me know he remembers who I was, who I am, and maybe doesn't hate that I came back.

The sound of forks and the distant purr of the radio fill the recovery silence. Mom refills his coffee, topping off my cup even though I barely touched the first round. The pancakes now look like wet cardboard, the smiley face long since erased by too much syrup and the slow saturation of guilt.

Dad dents a corner of the newspaper, folding it like he's building an argument. "People say things," he says, voice even. "Around town. They always will. You shouldn't let it decide what you do next."

Mom's hand comes to rest on mine again. "We know it wasn't your fault, Tess." She says it quietly, as if the walls might try to listen in. "The accident—"

"Can we not?" I blurt it out, sharper than I mean to, and both of them jerk a little—Dad surprised, Mom near to spilling her tea. The heaviness in my chest clamps down, squeezing out anything that might pass for dignity. "Just... it's over, okay? There's nothing to talk about. There's nothing to fix." I shove my self away from the table, the chair adding to the awkward noise that scrapes across the kitchen tile, the sound sharp and ungracious. My parents both flinch—again. Not much phases them, but I guess they weren't expecting a full-on tantrum at breakfast this morning.

Dad opens his mouth, but I'm already halfway across the kitchen, my hands balled tight at my sides and my face burning.

Whitney Houston's "Do You Hear What I Hear?" starts playing on the radio, and if I weren't so angry with myself I'd laugh at the melodramatic timing—like the universe can't resist rubbing it in.

Mom calls after me, her voice gentle, "Tess, I'm..." but I'm not ready for round two. I make a beeline for my favorite childhood hiding spot, slamming the door behind me before my mother's apology can finish its flight up the stairs to the attic.

Dust motes swirl in the pale morning light, and the attic air is sharp with cold—so cold I can see my breath curling in front of me. I pull my coat tighter around myself, though it does little to dull the chill creeping through my bones. The air is dense with past years: brittle tinsel, dusty wreaths, the sharp ghost of pine from an artificial tree still boxed and bandaged in yellowed tape. Light sneaks in through a circular window, carving bright slices across the piles of who-we-used-to-be. I edge past suitcases no one has opened since the Bush administration and the ancient exercise bike that doubled as my coat rack in high school. In the far corner the cardboard boxes have formed a skyline, labeled in my mom's careful, so-serious Sharpie: "CHRISTMAS DECOR," "TESS – HIGH SCHOOL," "PHOTO ALBUMS – SOMERSET." For lack of a better idea, I peel off the lid to the photo box, my fingers trembling—not just from the cold, but from the weight of the memories I'm about to face.

It's all here: Ugly sweaters in family portraits, my baby teeth grinning from behind gaps and braces, Dad sporting a thick mustache that, in some eras, was considered both attractive and a sign of status.

Mom had started scrapbooking once, but never made it past the first decade. The result is a chaos of baby pictures, candid birthday shots, a hundred blurry soccer poses, a thousand Christmas Eves, each year layered onto the next like sediment, or regret. I find a series of Polaroids from when I was seven: me dressed as a shepherd for the kids' nativity, bath towel knotted tight over my hair, gift-wrapped box at my feet. Dad's old arm in the shot, steadying my shoulder, his watch face glinting silver circles in the flash. I touch the picture, running my thumb over the faded colors, and wonder if I really was as happy then as I looked. Or if, even then, I knew how to fake it for everyone else's sake.

There's a photo of me and Brayden, eighth grade, both wearing matching Santa hats and the world's most awkward poses. I'd forgotten about this moment—until now. His arm around my shoulder, my face going beet red for the camera, both of us cheesing so hard our eyes had nearly vanished. It's right there in the flash, the way we leaned into each other. No space at all, and none needed.

Later, there was the year of the cast, my leg propped up on the living room ottoman while Brayden photo bombed from the background, a Santa hat sagging over one eyebrow. There's another, less staged: me and him, maybe fifteen, standing under the eaves at dusk while snow dusts his hair and mine, and the world behind us is washed out by porchlight and the glow of a distant star. I remember that night. We'd slipped away from the youth group Christmas bash, filched two cans of Coke from the cooler and dared each other to drink them in one go. He'd burped the alphabet, and I'd laughed so hard I'd sprayed half my can across the porch steps, practically doubled over. We'd both gotten an earful from Mrs. Keane when we trudged back in, cheeks pink with cold and sugar, still giggling.

I shuffle through the stack, the photos thinning out as the years go by. Prom, graduation, then nothing; a blank spot like the shadow left when you tape something to the window and the sun fades the rest. The years after high school stretched, elastic and empty, barely anything worth remembering except the fact that I left.

Closing the box, I lean my head back against the attic wall, the insulation scratchy through my hoodie and my eyes burning from more than dust.

Nobody ever talks about how nostalgia is both sweet and sad at the same time. The longer I stare at the old photos, the more it settles in—the quiet ache of what I left behind, and the deep, unshaken guilt of knowing I made my parents, Brayden, everyone, carry my absence with them through every holiday since.

Why did I come back? Mabel's question, sharp as ever. I thought it was just about Dad, about duty, maybe about avoiding what I didn't want to face in the city. A convenient excuse, I'm starting to see it's about something else entirely. Not running, not duty, not even the litany of things I'm still too scared to name. Maybe beneath it all, I just wanted some proof that it wasn't all a waste—that the years here, the people, the memories that refuse to die quietly, still meant something after I tried so hard to scrub them off my skin like preparing for surgery.

Trust yourself, trust the people who care about you, and trust the Lord, Mable had said. It hits me harder now, in the quiet of the attic, surrounded by boxes of my own history. The truth is, trusting the Lord—or anyone else—is harder when you can't even trust your own heart not to betray you.

I've spent the better part of forever double-checking every feeling, combing over my motives with tweezers and forceps like I'm searching for a tumor nobody else can see. No one's needed to keep my pride in check because I lead the league at self-inflicted guilt. I could win Olympic gold in beating myself up.

That's been true of me since the first time I realized I could disappoint someone I loved. After that, it was always easier to blame myself before anyone else got a chance. Preemptive strike, neat and tidy. It's the same with forgiveness—I'll hand it out like cookies to everyone but me. I could forgive Brayden for moving on, for staying in this town and turning out honest and good. I could forgive my parents for their worry, even the sharp edge of Dad's "You always have" this morning. But somewhere along the way, I decided that my own shame was immune to grace and that God couldn't forgive me.

I fold the photo of me-and-Brayden into a makeshift tent between my fingers. My head is full of the voices that have always bossed me around—Dad's strongest at the moment, but edged out at the last second by Mabel's gentle, infinite patience. Trust the Lord. Not a suggestion, apparently, but a line of code in my operating system. If I let myself believe in any of it, that God might actually want me to come crawling back to church with pockets full of cheap glitter and a heart that fails every medical exam for fitness or sincerity, would he even listen?

Seven

The church basement is a hive of fluorescent lights and mothball air, and when I duck through the door, I nearly trip over a stray tangle of extension cords. It's the kind of place where it's always winter—cold concrete, a single battered heater humming a lost hymn. The corner near the water heater is choked with cardboard boxes, bins labeled in marker: ANGELS, SHEPHERDS, JOSEPH/MISC. Someone's plugged in a little desk radio, static- coughing Mariah Carey's "All I Want for Christmas is You" at low volume. *I should've made stronger coffee.*

The folding tables are already full, covered in a colorful scatter of felt, polyester pipe cleaners, and the occasional stray halo from last year's clean-up. I set my bag carefully on a chair, having brushed the wet from my boots before stepping inside, though my eyes catch a small, spreading puddle near the end of a table where someone has clearly tracked snow in. It's the kind of thing that wouldn't have registered with me before—when I was younger, I'd have stepped right past without a thought. Now, after years in the city, it feels harder to ignore. *Have I become so particular?* The rhythm of the room is oddly familiar, voices overlapping, hands busy at work, the low hum of movement all around me.

I'm early, which would be relaxing if not for the fact that being alone in a church basement with people I don't know ranks just behind dentist's chairs and airport security on my list of anxiety triggers. Instead I busy myself with the nearest bin, excavating a collapsed Wise Man hat and enough shimmery gold fabric to wrap the entire cast. I don't need to check the tags to know they're probably repurposed candy wrappers and emergency blankets—but what Grace Hollow nativity ever made it through a dress rehearsal without at least one McGyvered costume moment? I dig until my hands turn metallic and my scalp tingles from the smell of tinsel.

The door at the top of the stairs blows open, letting in a cold draft and the sound of several people. I look up, and sure enough, it's Hannah and her son in tow, each carrying a tray of what look like... gingerbread sheep? Sure. I take a second to steel myself before greeting them, but Hannah's already in full teacher mode, rallying everyone with a whistle I forgot she could do.

"Don't mind us," she calls, balancing her sheep cookies like a pro. "We come bearing snacks and a total absence of judgment," she crowed, dropping the sheep cookies onto the table in front of me.

Her son, Ben, doesn't so much set his tray down as let it crash- land, and promptly disappears to the corner where the bins of plastic swords and foam spears live.

A couple more volunteers trickle in behind her, rounding out the cast of usual suspects—Mrs. Keane with a basket of thread, Jeff from the hardware store in a fluorescent beanie, and one of the high school girls, Angela, who immediately launches into a story about how she's definitely not doing the donkey costume this year. "I wore it last year and the inside still smells like Doritos and a sub," she says, and I believe her.

She eyes me, then the sheep cookies, then the heap of garland, before running off to the opposite end of the table. I can't even blame her.

Hannah dives in with the kind of energy you need to run Bible school and single-parenthood at once: "Tess, could you help me rip these into strips?" she says, not waiting for my answer, pushing a bolt of blue velvet my way. I shrug off my coat and start working, grateful for something to do with my hands. The next few minutes are a blur of scissors, tangled ribbons, and harmless gossip flying over our heads with the wild freedom of unsupervised Sunday Schoolers.

The chatter pulls me in and I let the monotony of cutting velvet ease me into the crowd. It should feel strange, being back in this particular circle of church-busywork, but it's so automatic that I catch myself humming along to Mariah before I know it.

Within a few minutes the table is a war zone of blue fluff and discarded end pieces. Hannah shoots me a grateful grin. "I knew you were a ringer," she says. "I put you on Angel One and Mary's helper, FYI."

"I thought I'd be a wise man," I shoot back with my most serious face, which cracks immediately.

"You're too short for a beard," says Hannah, not missing a beat. "Also, nobody trusts you with the frankincense after what happened in fourth grade."

I wrinkle my nose. I do remember. The frankincense— actually flammable citronella, the glitter, and the sparklers—an unholy trinity that guaranteed there would never be open flames in Nativity again.. "I regret nothing."

"You say that now, but wait until you're stuck in a polyester tunic two sizes too small," Hannah teases, and for a second, it almost feels like it used to. Like I'm fourteen again with my surrogate little sister by my side, warping our voices with helium from the altar arrangement and plotting how to get the baby Jesus to say "ga-ga" during dress rehearsal.

Mrs. Keane, who must've heard every word, offers a tight- lipped smile as she threads a needle. "We still haven't gotten the scorch marks out of the carpet," she says, but I catch the crinkle in her eyes and know it's more fond than furious.

The new angel costumes come together faster than I expected. Maybe it's muscle memory, or maybe it's just that I've always been an Olympic-level overachiever when it comes to Christmas crafts. Either way, the table starts to look celebratory instead of tragic by the time the next batch of volunteers stumbles in, trailing slush and Chex Mix in their wake.

During a rare lull I spot Brayden at the top of the stairs, arms loaded with a lopsided stack of pageant props and, somehow, still managing to balance a mug of coffee on top. He looks even taller with the props, the quiet hum of activity around him making the moment oddly still. For a split second, I'm on the brink of saying something—it's a reflex, that urge to fill the space between us. Always was. But the words stick, and I just watch as he sets down the stack, surveys the scene, and grins in quiet surrender.

"Hope you like chaos," he says, the smile audible in his voice. "I work in an ER," I remind him. "This is practically a yoga retreat."

Brayden's laugh is a little shy but genuine, and he shakes his head like he's not used to being outmatched. He gets busy with the duct tape and cardboard, and I pretend not to notice when he keeps glancing over, like he's checking to see if I'll bolt again. I channel all my buzz into the angel wings, toggling back and forth between glue gun triage and monitoring the slow encroachment of gingerbread sheep into every available inch of table space.

The conversation finds me anyway. First small talk—holidays, the ice on Main Street, whether the high school band will survive the incoming principal. But then, like moss creeping over stone, nostalgia works its way in. Hannah brings up the year the pageant donkey pooped on stage (twice), and someone else remembers the blizzard that stranded the entire cast in the church for a full day.

Mrs. Keane had made hot cocoa on a camp stove and all the shepherds got sick from eating nothing but marsh-mallows and communion wafers. We laugh about it, the story growing more outlandish with each embellishment, and it's a relief to see that the past can be reimagined just by telling it together. Even Angela, mid-Gen Z and glued to her phone, smirks with something like pride when someone brings up the time she split her pants at dress rehearsal.

The longer we work, the more I let down my guard. I start to remember the rhythm of these moments: the joke that never dies, the way Hannah can read my mood in a glance, the scrape of scissors and the slap of tape as their own kind of music. Even the tension in my shoulders starts to loosen. I'm still the outsider, the prodigal daughter returned, but here—with my hands full of pipe cleaners and felt, surrounded by people who mostly remember me as I was—I can almost believe I have a place.

Brayden floats to the edge of the group, tape in hand and a fleck of gold fabric on his cheekbone. He's always been like that: comfortable being needed, less comfortable being the center of attention. I remember that from before—the times he'd orchestrate elaborate pranks at youth group only to vanish when they went spectacularly well or horrifyingly sideways. The more things change.

He stops beside me, tilting his head thumb-ward toward the water heater. "Hey, Doc, can I steal you for a minute?"

I somehow swallow the ridiculous spike in blood pressure that comes from him using my old nickname, the one he gave me way back in grade school because of Dad being the town doctor and my obsession with the seven dwarves, but my voice is only a little squeaky when I say, "Sure, Reverend."

He grins at the volley, then jerks his head for me to follow. I set down my shears, brush the angel fuzz off my hands, and trail after him down past the rows of storage. The further we get from the project epicenter, the quiet thickens, until it's just the low hum of the heater and the echo of our footsteps on the concrete. We're out of sight of the others, in the nook by the water heater where a single folding chair sags beneath the weight of a hefty box labeled SETS: 1998-2022. In spite of the warmth of the room, the cold cement seeps up through my boots.

Brayden leans against the cinderblock wall, arms folded, his eyes on the ceiling like he's searching for divine help in untangling whatever he's about to say. I tuck my hands in my pockets and wait. He's always taken his time winding up to the hard stuff, and I'm content to let the silence fill up first. It's easier than pretending I don't notice the way he still drums two fingers against his bicep when he's nervous.

"Didn't mean to make things weird at the pageant rehearsal," he says at last, voice low. His mouth tilts—half-annoyed, half- deflection. "I thought maybe we'd just... pick up where we left off. Didn't think about how it'd be for you."

His apology lands heavier than I expect. I breathe out slowly. "You didn't do anything wrong," I say, and I mean it. For the first time in what feels like years, I actually mean it. "I'm just—bad at old friends."

"Lucky I'm not that old yet."

He kicks gently at the baseboard, and I swear he's fighting the urge to fidget more. The hallway light is dim, but I can see him searching my face for some hint of an answer I'm not sure I have.

He tries again. "I never expected you to come back. Like, not really."

"Me neither," I say.

There's a sound from the far side of the basement props box. The thunk echoes across the room, scattering the thread of conversation. I look at him, really look, and for the first time since I'd driven back into Maple Ridge, I see the worry underneath his face—the lines on his forehead I don't remember.

We both laugh, all at once, maybe just to cut the tension, and the sound is so normal and so much like before that I forget for a second that anything ever changed. But it did. We both know it.

"I'm normally good at this," he says, scratching the back of his head as if it might steady him. "Talking and...stuff." He clears his throat, glances away, then back again. "I guess what I'm trying to say is..." He hesitates, the words catching somewhere between thought and breath. "I'm glad you came back, even if it's just for the pageant. It's good seeing you here."

I nod, slipping my hands deeper into my pockets, as if hiding my restless thoughts could make them quieter. "It's weird," I admit, because part of me still wants to find a way to fit him into my life—just a little—though I've spent years convincing myself I didn't need to.

He shifts his weight, letting his boot scrape softly against the floor. "We were a good team, though," he says finally, like he's rehearsed it, even though it comes out soft and honest. "You made Christmas interesting."

"That's one way to say it," I say, but the smile that escapes is real. "It's not like the place fell apart without me."

Brayden casts me a sideways glance, a faint smile tugging at one corner of his mouth. "Maybe not," he says, "but they did have to triple the fire insurance."

I snort, a laugh breaking free before I can stop it, the sound tangles with a rush of memory. "You're the one who built a bonfire out of old Bibles, Pastor."

His forehead creases as he tries to play innocent. "That was a deeply theological point about the Light of Christ."

"Oh, sure. And getting the youth group to make s'mores behind the church was...?"

He tips his chin. "Evangelism, obviously." His eyes flick up to meet mine, and we laugh together for a moment. If I could have bottled this sound when I was away, I might never have missed Maple Ridge so much.

We slip into a silence that draws out longer than it should. Brayden's clearly holding something back, the way he always did before dropping big news. He shifts against the wall, rubs his hands together, and then glances at me sidelong, blue eyes bright but anchored to something serious.

"You ever think about it?" he asks, almost too softly. I blink, unsure what "it" means—until I see the way he's looking at me, past me, toward all the years I ran from this building and the God who supposedly lived in it.

He presses on, maybe afraid I'll run. "Faith, I mean. Church. You ever wonder if..." he drags his thumb along the joint of his knuckle, gathering courage, "any of this stuff still means anything after everything that's happened?"

I freeze, not sure if he means what happened in town, or what happened to us, or the entire last decade. I wait for him to add more, but he just lets the question hover.

The pipes above us groan—old plumbing, or maybe the ghosts of all the dumb things we said in this church growing up. I try to answer without sounding like I'm diagnosing a patient.

"I guess so." I clear my throat, and it comes out anxious and uncertain. "I think about it sometimes...I guess." I force a shrug, pretending it's no big deal. "Work, city life, you know how it is. It's just...I got busy."

I know it's the oldest, lamest excuse. Brayden's too tactful to call it out, but I can feel the disappointment just below his outer calm. I want to tell him what he wants to hear— that I never really lost the faith, that I miss it, that when I hear someone pray for a sick loved one it makes the world feel less like it's spinning off its axis. It would be easier, in a way, to just say I still believe with my whole, unfractured heart. That coming here is a step toward something holier and not just a desperate, nostalgic, attempt to rewrite the past. Part of me even wants to give him the answer he's looking for, not because I owe it to him, but because I want him to think I'm still a person who deserves to be here, to be missed, to maybe even be forgiven for falling away.

"I got busy" is not the whole truth, and Brayden knows it. His gaze sharpens—not in judgment, but concern—and for a fraction of a second I want to bite my own tongue off for sounding so empty-handed.

He doesn't let me squirm. "Maybe...or," he says, so quiet I almost don't catch it. "You got hurt."

There's nothing accusatory in his voice. If anything, it's offered like a gentle diagnosis—one I've denied so long I barely know it's there. But something unspools in my chest, raw and surprised, and before I can blink it away, Brayden just... reaches for my hand. Like we're still kids. Like it's the most natural thing in the world.

His palm is warm and strange, callused just enough to feel real, not holy. The pressure is a little awkward, but comforting and there's enough heat in it that my lungs forget how to fill. I look down at our joined hands—his thumb tracing a careful arc over my knuckles, grounding me in this moment as if nothing else exists. It's the most innocent thing and the most dangerous, because I remember exactly what it was to have him in my corner. To want it again.

I swallow and try to speak, but the words tangle themselves up somewhere between my heart and my mouth. Brayden must sense this, because he holds on a second longer, squeezing my hand just once before letting go. It's the same gesture he always used after I'd bombed on a school test—one gentle squeeze, one look that meant it was okay, I was okay. I'm fighting to keep my face together, my eyes fixed on the floor, when a sharp voice cuts through the charged quiet.

"I hope I'm not interrupting anything...private."

There is only one person in Maple Ridge who could weaponize the word 'private' mid-morning in a church basement. The look she gives us is straight-up surgical, slicing the air between Brayden and me faster than a scalpel through a ham. I jerk my hand away, cheeks blazing, but he recovers with an ease that should be illegal.

"Nancy! Didn't hear you coming down," Brayden says, voice back to its usual Pastor Mode—calm, open, just a little too loud. "You need something?"

She drops the box down hard on the nearest chair, then smooths the wrinkles out of her coat sleeve with a deliberate, unhurried motion. "Oh, I see you're busy."

She doesn't look at me, not directly, but her expression feels pointed. "Some of the pageant parents are here with questions. I assumed you'd want to greet them, Pastor?" she says, her tone carrying a quiet edge.

Brayden gives me an apologetic, almost helpless look that's so familiar my pulse skips. "Go ahead," I say, all clinical distance, but my voice comes out weirdly flat. "I should get back to costuming."

He watches me for a second, maybe expecting another word or a glimmer of the old me, but all I can do is clutch the edges of my pockets and wait for him to turn away.

When he does, I spin a hundred and eighty degrees and head straight for the stairs, nearly knocking over the box marked PROPS: 2013-2017 in my rush to exit.

The cement floor amplifies my footsteps as I hurriedly dash up the stairs, taking them two at a time. I slam my fist against the door and burst into the blinding sunlight and icy air. *Great, I'm running again.*

Eight

I t takes less than a day for the entire town of Maple Ridge to know my shoe size, my coffee order, and the precise timestamp of the little 'moment' I shared with Brayden "Pastor" James. Oh, the scandal. It's practically printed in the local Gazette, under the world's least flattering photo of me running out of the church basement in shame. By the time I make it to Shady's General Store the old ghosts are clinging to my side like long lost friends whispering how indiscreet I am. Every person I pass by pretends not to recognize me, except for the elderly man at the entrance of the store who gives me an exaggerated wink that probably means I should be flattered, but mostly makes my ears burn.

I clutch a basket full of garland and costume-safe white face paint while humming along to "Rockin' Around the

Christmas Tree" by Brenda Lee, trying to decide how far the church budget will stretch. My head's still buzzing from that whole ordeal, where I showed great restraint when I didn't smack the Holy Spirit right out of Nancy Miller. I can't believe I let her rattle me like that. *I work in an ER!*

I duck down the baking aisle, praying the shelves will act as a barricade against the town's collective hive mind. But behind the display of Christmas cookie cutters, I hear them: two voices, one acid-sweet and unmistakable.

"She just shows up, after all these years?" Nancy Miller, Queen of Grace Hollow's morals and self-appointed gossip honoree of Maple Ridge. The woman could weaponize a prayer chain faster than I can take a patient's blood pressure. She's wrapped in a heavy floral wool coat over a pastel cardigan, her neck wrapped in a crocheted scarf, and her sensible boots planted firmly as if bracing against both the cold and the weight of everyone's business.

"Well, I think it's brave," says the other, a breathy voice I couldn't begin to recall from my past life, "coming back to help with the children's pageant. I heard she's a doctor now. Emergency medicine, maybe? Always was a bit dramatic."

"I never could," Nancy says, her tone tinged with something between disapproval and concern. "But we ought to pray for her, of course." A clipped pause follows, as if she's on a call with God and expects Him to pick up right away.

I'm about to make my escape when I hear them stop in mid conversation and move in my direction. Nancy rounds the end of the display, bumping her basket conspicuously into mine so that a box of Grape-nuts Cereal falls to the floor. I stoop to retrieve it—reflex, muscle memory, and catch her eye as I hand it over. Her gratitude is practiced, like the pleasantries she's been rehearsing since she could tie a bow. "Thank you, Tess," she says, loud enough for the entire shelf of baking goods to bear witness. "I was just telling Emily how much we appreciate you coming back."

I manage a smile, but it's got more teeth than warmth. "I aim to please," I say, turning to pull a tub of cookie icing from the shelf. As if I was daring her to show more sweetness than me, Nancy closes the gap, lowering her voice just enough to make it sound juicy, "I think it's wonderful you're involved with church again. I told the ladies' group you'd fit right in."

That's when Emily, who is dressed in all beige, leans in close and says, "We're all just so glad to see you, Tess." She means it, but she's also absolutely desperate for details.

Nancy's lips part, and for a wild second I think she's actually going to ask me about Brayden. I brace myself for the kind of question you only hear in a police interrogation room, but she fakes me out—her real topic is so much more boring. "Do you think the pageant will even work this year?" she asks, twisting the lid off her skepticism and pouring it thick. "The new budget, the recent renovations, the heating—did you know about the heating? Of course not, you've only just come back."

I decide that the only way through is forward. "Hannah's been doing a great job organizing everything," I say, letting my voice ring out with just enough edge to draw a couple of rubberneckers from the end of the aisle. "If anyone can make the pageant work, it's her."

That gets Nancy's eyebrows to rise right into her perfectly curled bangs. "Of course, but you can see how it's...well, different, for someone who's not been involved for so long. Church traditions are hard to step right back into." She offers a bright, brittle smile that feels less like a welcome mat and more like a warning sign. "And, dear, you've got such important medical work in the city. Wouldn't you rather focus on things you're... more suited to?"

I clench the icing tub so hard the lid almost buckles. "You'd be surprised what I'm suited to, Nancy," I say without looking away. The edge in my voice should warn her off, but it only makes Nancy's smile brighten, as if she's just won a round she wasn't even supposed to be playing.

She cocks her head, lowering her voice to an urgent little whisper. "Oh, I'm not doubting you, dear. You've always been... talented." She clings to the word like it's as suspicious as it is flattering. "It's just, with your history and all, I worry that Grace Hollow's unique demands might be a bit...intense. For someone just coming back, you know...after what happened."

The air chills, and I feel myself sliding toward the edge of reason. Nothing gets my blood pressure up quite like an attempt at armchair psychoanalysis from someone whose credentials are in social media gossip. But Nancy, God bless her, is relentless.

She leans a little closer, voice dipped in honey but designed to sting. "You can understand how some might think you're rushing it, coming back like this," she says, tilting her head just enough to look earnest. "We wouldn't want an...issue, at the wrong time. Or for it to drag down the Pastor."

There it is. The invisible line, crossed with a stiletto heel and a smile.

I hear my own voice drop, tighter than a tourniquet. "I'm sure the Pastor can handle himself," I say, and the word 'Pastor' slips out far sharper than intended. If Nancy notices, she's undeterred.

"Oh, but can he?" she says. "You know," her voice goes confessional, "after all the work he's done to build trust... I'd just hate for hard memories to bubble up again. For either of you." She pats my forearm with the kind of practiced care reserved for ICU patients and fragile egos. "We only want what's best for you, dear."

Something in my chest cracks, and I swear, for the briefest second, I see my hand lifting, ready to deliver the world's most satisfying slap to the epitome of Sunday-morning sanctimony.

It's not even anger, really. Just this thunderclap of tiredness. Tired of being dissected, tired of the gossip-network, tired of the tilted heads and the "we just care" act that runs on a loop in this town. I can taste my own pulse, that sourness on the back of my tongue.

I am three seconds from giving Nancy a new prayer request for next Sunday when a voice interrupts—low, warm, measured, and close enough to carry the promise of rescue. "Is this where the Christmas spirit is hiding today, ladies?"

Brayden. Thirty-two years of maple syrup and hayrides and church basements and somehow he can still disarm a landmine without breaking stride. He stands at the end of the aisle, hands tucked in his jacket pockets, smile aimed right between me and Nancy like a white flag. The sight of him just about saves me from committing a felony.

Nancy's expression shifts so seamlessly I'm actually in awe. "Pastor Brayden!" she sings, full of fake delight. "We were just catching up with Tess—so good of you to join us."

He wastes zero time, gliding over with a pastor's experience and a practiced friend's concern. "Glad I caught you both," he says, nodding at Nancy before giving me a look that's equal parts rescue rope and apology. "Is there a problem I can help with?"

Nancy shuffles her cereal box like a shield, her smile going a few shades more brittle. "Oh no, Pastor…I was just telling Tess, " Nancy goes on, "how much we appreciate her help, despite her…hectic schedule."

The look Brayden gives her is diplomatic, but his hand finds my shoulder in gentle, unspoken solidarity and I feel, not for the first time, that he might be the only person on earth who could talk me down from a high ledge.

Nancy clocks the casual touch, registers the gentle squeeze, and her entire posture pivots from predatory to placating in a single inhale. She gathers herself. "Well, I won't keep you, then," she chirps at Brayden, which is church-lady code for "let's pretend this never happened."

She flashes a smile at both of us before snagging Emily and heading towards the register, chattering away.

The silence Nancy leaves in her wake is almost a vacuum, but Brayden's presence brings the oxygen right back. He lets his hand linger on my shoulder a second longer, then drops it, clearing his throat. "You doing okay?" he asks, voice softer than "Do They Know it's Christmas," by Band Aid, humming overhead.

I nod, but it's a lie. "Didn't think I'd need crowd control training just to buy sprinkles."

He offers a crooked smile, softer than usual. "Nancy's been training for this moment since junior high. You handled her better than most."

"Well, she just never gave up her roll as head mean-girl from high school," I say, still trying to stop my hands from shaking.

He glances over at my cart. "Is this a supply raid, or are you preparing for a glitter-based siege?"

"Little of both," I say, pushing the cart into motion. "The pageant's a mess. Mrs. Keane's sheep are fighting the Wisemen, the angel wings are held together with prayer and duct tape, and Hannah's threatening to go on strike. We're all going to need therapy by Saturday."

He laughs, that nice, easy sound. "Isn't that what Christmas is about? Disaster, duct tape, and hope?"

I shoot him a look. "And forgiveness?"

"Definitely," he says. "Can I walk with you? Or is that against pageant protocol?"

I hesitate, then nod. "Just don't let Nancy catch us holding hands or she'll start an inquisition."

He gives this small, honest laugh, and for a second I wonder if the whole town feels as suffocating to him as it does to me. We meander through the isles. He doesn't rush, just falls into step, letting the quiet fill up our ears until it almost feels normal.

Then, like he's been sitting on the thought for a while, Brayden says, "You know, after everything that happened, I never thought I'd end up...here." He gestures with the edge of a smile at the store, the lights, the aisle draped in fake tinsel and plastic snowmen. "Not Maple Ridge, I mean...just, doing what I do. Being who I am. A pastor."

I don't answer right away. I'm still busy sorting the new puzzle that is Brayden James: old friend, one-time co-conspirator, resurrected as Maple Ridge's unlikely spiritual leader and, apparently, emotional bomb squad. I fish for a good reply, and my brain latches onto his profile, the curve of his jaw and how it tenses, how his mouth purses to tell a joke but doesn't.

I place a box of cocoa into my basket. "Yeah, the 'pastor' thing's new for me, too. So...what changed?" I ask, and I'm not fishing for the polite, Sunday School answer. I want to know the real reason, the one he tells himself at two in the morning when the town is asleep and the past is louder than sleep.

He shrugs, hands in his pockets, studying the shelves of cake mix like they hold the secret. "I used to think I'd never fit here. You remember." He glances at me, and the hint of the old troublemaker sparkles in his blue eyes. "But after you left, I tried the big city...and all the things we used to dream about." He laughs, but there's a catch in it. "Turns out, I was way better at rebellion than you."

I snort. He's exaggerating, I set the gold standard for small- town rebellion, and everyone knew it. If there was a rule, I'd break it. If there was a boundary, I'd tiptoed across it and left muddy up and down the sidewalk just to say I had.

He catches my look and grins, as if reading my mind. "Yeah. I know. But here's the secret...out there, all the pushing and proving and never looking back? It was just noise. I spent a lot of late nights alone thinking... maybe I was just... broken. I couldn't claw my way out of the bottle I crawled into. I finally stopped trying."

We head down the next aisle, the lights bright enough to make his words feel even more real. "I used to hate it when people started talking about forgiveness or re-demption, because I thought it was just a word you threw around when you screwed up too publicly to hide. But, it's more personal than that. A walk...to be sure. But personal."

He stops at the end of the aisle, turning to look at me, and for a second we're the only two people in this garland-choked universe, faces washed out in the fluo-rescents, serenaded by Elvis' "Blue Christmas" piped in from the ceiling.

"Sometime in the middle of the night, in the middle of Chicago's Pacific Garden Mission, when I had given up all hope, a man started talking to me about hope. His name was Tom Bauer. He changed my life." He laughs again, a little self-conscious, it doesn't quite reach the surface, but his eyes are steady. "He told me, 'You're not meant to save yourself. Christ already did it.' And I thought, sure, that's the kind of thing you say to get a guy off a bridge or out of a bottle." Brayden shrugs, like that should be the punchline, but there's more.

"I'd been to church my whole life," he says, "but it never stuck. Not really. I thought God was just—rules, and guilt, and keeping up appearances for people like Nancy. But Tom...he made it sound like grace was real. Like it was for people who already knew they couldn't ever measure up."

Brayden's voice dips, even softer. "For most of my teens...and even into my early twenties, I thought God wanted me to just... keep cleaning up my own mess. Like I had to get it all perfect before He'd want anything to do with me. It wasn't until I finally bottomed out, Tess, that I realized that's not the deal." He stops, searching for words. "Tom was the first person who ever looked at me and said, 'God knows you, Bray. He Knows the worst...and He Still wants you.'" His eyes find mine, and I can see in them the rawness of his memories. "And he meant it." He shrugs, the motion small, but tender. "I gave my life to Christ that night. I mean, actually gave it. Not just at camp or youth group or on some emotional summer week where you come home and nothing sticks. This time, it stuck. Anyway, that's how I started the journey that brought me...here."

I can't respond. I can't even find a breath. He's not being dramatic—he's being Brayden, at his most disarmingly honest. I grip my basket against the ache in my chest that is causing my arms to turn to rubber.

"I didn't know any of that, " I say. It comes out softer than I meant, and my eyes are starting to sting, right there by the shelf of instant oatmeal. Not because Brayden turned into a pastor or even because he found his redemption, but because I'm realizing what a black hole I was to everyone who ever got too close. The guilt I thought I'd left in the attic comes roaring back, a shame-spiral in Technicolor. I'd always seen myself as the one who needed fixing, the one who ran away, but I never really looked hard at what I'd left behind when I did.

I swipe away the tears that are forming and keep my eyes down, focusing on balancing the items in my basket. Even though Brayden probably notices, he says nothing, and it's the best thing he can do. He just waits, grounded and solid, anchoring me while a storm spins in my head.

My fingers have stopped trembling with anger and are now shaking for some other reason entirely. I don't trust myself to let the feeling out, so I force a dry laugh. "Well. That sure beats my first week in New York City, which mostly involved apartment mold and a neighbor who thought New York-style pizza was a love language."

Brayden grins, but he's not letting me off the hook. "You always did talk about running away to find something bigger. Did you?"

I want to say yes. I want to tell him about the residency and the all-nighters and the times the hospital coffee tasted worse than hotdog water from a downtown cart in July, and those sunrise walks home in someone else's city, and the one New Year's Eve I spent stitching a drunk Santa's eyebrow back together while the world counted down without me. I want to tell him, of course I found something bigger. But looking at Brayden, what he's made of himself and the peace that sits on his shoulders like he finally knows how to wear it, I can't remember the last time I ever felt anything remotely like belonging.

"Guess I'm still looking," I admit, and the words come out so thin and honest they almost vanish in the aisle air.

There's something in his gaze that makes me want to tell him every ugly, unfinished thing about myself. Maybe that's why it hurts. I didn't come back to Maple Ridge to unpack my insides. I came to patch up my dad, rescue my mom from her worry, and coast through the holiday under the radar. I did not come for confession. I did not come to measure myself against the person I used to be, or the people I hurt along the way.

If he said the right thing right now, I'd probably detonate in a cascade of confessions and ugly sobs and all the things I have spent the last thirteen years pretending didn't matter. Instead, he just stands there, letting the moment soften and spread, keeping me company in the mess.

I stare so hard at the instant oatmeal that I nearly blur the expiration date right off the box. Something brittle lingers just under my skin, begging for release—for a fight, a scream, a prayer. If I let him see it, he'd never forget. I will myself to hold it in.

Brayden doesn't push. He just waits for me to compose myself as I shift my basket again. *It's getting heavy.* I hate how hard it is to breathe, with all the old ghosts closing in.

He glances at the basket, at my hands, then into my eyes. "I'm glad you're back," he says.

Nine

There's magic in the sound of children singing badly—it's the only time chaos feels like hope.

Tonight, the sanctuary is in shadow while the stage is glowing gold – dust motes whirling in the spotlights that catch the angel wings and wise men robes in song. At the front, Hannah waves her conductor's hand with all the authority of a cruise ship captain steering through a nor'easter. The children are equal parts mutiny and miracle, all sweaty from all the running around.

I lean in the doorway, coat still zipped to my chin, counting how many halos are listing to one side. (Four. Five, if you count the baby cherub who keeps eating his own tinsel.) No one notices me, and I bask in it—just a shadow at the edge, neither star nor scandal, yet.

Brayden cuts a path along the pews, untangling a squabble between two shepherds and repairing a broken staff with scotch tape and a look that says, I've seen worse. He's so in his element it's almost annoying. He catches my eye, tips a half-salute, then kneels to tie a Wise Man's loose sandal with careful attention. I watch him for too long, a thousand headlines from Nancy Miller assembling in my brain, all variations on "Fallen Angel Returns for Salvation (or Hot Pastor?)"

Hannah spies me at last, her voice slicing through "O Come, All Ye Faithful" with a welcome relief. "Tess! You're right on time. We need an extra hand with the wings. And maybe some herding with the sheep...Ben's hiding behind the manger again." I consider feigning sickness, but she's already on me, thrusting a glue gun and a tray of donut holes as if she expects me to glue the children in place. "We're modeling a spirit of hospitality," she stage-whispers.

A tiny, sugared hand tugs my sleeve. Ben, doughnut powder dusting the front of his red-striped shirt, stares up at me with the seriousness of a doctor diagnosing a problem. "I think the real Baby Jesus would have had Lego's in his crib," he says, and I nod my full, professional agreement.

"I'm not qualified to argue that," I tell him with a wink.

He blinks, then breaks into a sweet grin.

For the briefest, oddest moment, I picture what that world would look like—a whole nativity set built from mismatched Lego, Mary, Joseph and baby Jesus immortalized as tiny Minifigs. *Wow, that would upset the old-folks!*

"Ben, you're up for Bethlehem star next!" Hannah calls. He zips away, dropping donut holes in his wake. Less kid angel, more comet streak—he rockets up the steps to center stage and collides with the Wise Men in a glorious tangle of robes and glitter. The entire front row dissolves into giggles. It's exactly as I remember from when I was a kid, right down to the frayed carpet under the first pew and the ancient radiator clanking protest during every quiet moment.

I lose sight of Brayden until he appears at my elbow, voice softer than the chaos warrants. "Did you get a chance to look over the program?" he asks, but before I can answer, a small herd of children stampedes the aisle and swarm him like he's Santa at a Black Friday toy drop. They beg for reruns on the lighting cues, for extras on the treat table, for the chance to swap costumes because someone "doesn't want to be a camel anymore, camels are boring." Brayden's grin never wavers, not even when one of the angel wings whacks him in the face.

He's a natural, a shepherd to the little flock in every sense of the word. I watch him kneel to the smallest girl, patch her glittery belt, and speak quiet encouragement that settles her stage fright by a full decibel.

"I read it over," I say, laughing at how out of place I feel. "Twice. Thankfully, most of the kids have more lines than me." Brayden smiles, reassurance reflecting in his eyes. "Most of them," he says, "but you're the only one who won't freeze if the sound system implodes mid-song." He lowers his voice. "Or if someone sets the props table on fire, again."

I roll my eyes. "We agreed never to speak of the frankincense incident."

Before I could say more, a tug at my sleeve makes me turn. The cherub with the tinsel-eating habit is swaying on his heels, face pinched in deep, comical concern.

"Are you a real doctor?" he asks, voice so high it nearly vibrates the donut tray.

I glance at Hannah, who shrugs, as if to say, "You field this one;" and then, at Brayden.

He presses his lips to stifle a laugh. "Depends who's asking," he says, reading hesitation in my eyes.

The cherub rubs one chubby wrist, eyes huge and round as the moon. "My dad said you ran away to the big city because you didn't like church anymore," he blurts out, spraying a fine mist of donut sugar across my jeans. "But my mom says that's not true. She says sometimes people just get busy or sad."

For a second, my mouth opens and closes like a fish out of water, and I feel every adult within earshot pretend to focus harder on what they're doing.

"Do you actually live in a big city? With elevators and a subway...and everything?" His eyes actually get wider, looking for confirmation.

Brayden, ever my knight in shining armor, lowers himself to meet the boy's gaze. "Oh yes, elevators and everything. But you know what, buddy? Elevators aren't as fun as they seem. You miss out on all the adventures you can have playing in the woods or by the lake." With a gentle nudge and a smile at me, he encourages the little angel to go join his friends.

I watch the cherub run off, tinsel trailing behind him like a kite tail, and try to pretend that his words aren't bouncing around my head. I want to shake it off. I want to laugh like Brayden does, at how *kids will say anything*, but the truth is, the little voice hit its mark. I look up and spot Mabel across the sanctuary, corralling a squad of baby angels into a photo pose. She catches my eyes and gives a thumbs up, but I see the question behind it. Maybe everyone else does, too.

I realize, abruptly, that all these people have been living with the vacuum I left behind. Not just Brayden—with his quiet steadiness and his changed life, but every one of these kids, parents, and pageant marshals. The goofy rehearsals, the glue- gun crises, the fraying traditions that kept getting shabbier and funnier in my absence. I abandoned all of them when I bailed on this place and never looked back.

I watch Hannah wrangle the stage with a smile that's just a little brittle at the corners. I see how Mabel's laughter rings out a touch too loud, filling empty spaces. Even the parents— tired, patient, running interference with the siblings in the back pews—work in a world that used to include me, like I'm a ghost that went 'poof,' and left it all behind.

I grip the edge of the props table, throat tight, as the music winds down and Hannah calls for a break. The children scatter instantly, wings askew, robes trailing, their feet loud on the wooden floors. I stand there, knees locked, while the grownups flock to their stations—cider, cookies, the endless cycle of cleanup and crisis management.

Brayden finds me, leaning his hip next to mine at the props table, gaze soft but unwavering. "Sometimes I wonder how we got so old," he says under his breath. Something in his voice, gentle, half a joke but mostly not, makes my own pulse slow, then hitch.

I push a stray donut crumb in a slow circle, buying time. "Would it be weird to say I always figured everyone here just... paused when I left?" I say, the words came out of me before I realized they sounded cringe.

Brayden glances at the riot of children, whooping and chasing each other around the stage. "You should see the way they talk about you. Half the kids now want to be doctors or actresses, or at least live somewhere with an elevator. Everyone else...well, I think they'd like you to believe you never really left."

His words are meant as comfort, but instead they tunnel straight through me with the kind of clinical accuracy that makes me want to run a full battery of tests on my own soul. I swallow, thickly, and look out across the sanctuary. In every corner, some unpredictable bit of life is pinging wildly.

Instead, recalling the debacle at the general store, I retort, "Yeah, not exactly everyone shares your...optimism." I wave a hand. "Case-in-point: Nancy and her army of prayer warriors. I'm pretty sure she started a betting pool on how long before I set foot inside an actual Sunday service again."

Brayden grins, but it fades. "It's a very small town...and you know how some people get when they have something new to talk about."

I *do*. And standing here, watching the echoes of my absence play out in awkward nostalgia and tiny, sugar-fueled confessions, I finally see it wasn't just my parents or Brayden who got left behind. I was a hole that other people had to work around. I was the jigsaw piece that vanished and left everyone else rearranging to fill the gap, re-cutting themselves to fit the same picture.

A sudden rush of emotion catches me off guard, slicing neat and cold through the haze of donut glaze and pageant nostalgia. I exhale, trying to make a joke of it, but my voice skips a little. "I thought running away was the right thing at the time, but now...."

Brayden must sense the spiral, because his hand covers mine, warm and steady.

"You don't have to explain to me. Change is hard, and sometimes you have to go find what you're looking for, even if it hurts. We all have our own path to walk...our own lessons to learn."

The warmth of his hand steadies me, but all I can think is how out-of-place mine looks under his, how the city polish and the starchy coat sleeve piles so awkwardly beside his work-rough fingers, the smudge of pen from some earlier project. I want to pull away, and I want to never let go. Complicated, as ever.

"I guess what I'm saying," I manage, "I didn't realize how many unanswered questions I left behind. Or that I even... mattered." Even as I say it, the words taste strange. They aren't bitter, but hollow and uncertain.

His lips press together as if to answer but, around us, the kids ripple laughter through the aisles, chasing each other and the crumbs of their own excitement.

A squabble near the piano draws Brayden's attention. "If you'll excuse me, I think the camels are staging a coup." He gives my hand the gentlest squeeze before backing away, shepherding the peace with the patience of a saint. I watch him go, shoulders relaxed and voice kind, and try to commit the image to memory. Brayden, in his own world, fully himself.

I find myself taking refuge behind the curve of the props table, absently picking crusted glue from my fingers, wishing I could shed the years just as easily. From this safe haven, I watch the chaos unfold, feeling both drawn to and repelled by the energy. After a moment of hesitation and a deep breath, I finally muster the courage to step out into the fray, unsure about my place in any of this.

After everyone shuffles into the night, parents, restless kids, the core volunteers, Brayden is still inside in a conference with Hannah, and I take the opportunity to slip out the side door. The air is brutal, a slap of January in mid-December, my ears instantly numb.

The parking lot is blanketed in white, with red tail lights flickering in the distance and the silhouette of the church's white steeple against the star-filled night sky.

The Jeep is an igloo, but once I've cleared the glass the best I can with my sleeve—grumbling under my breath that the rental should've come with a snow scraper. I *should've picked one up somewhere.* I crank the heat and it becomes its own little sanctuary. I sit there, fingers tingling back to life, replaying the evening in fragments. In the dark, with the engine humming, it's easy to imagine that no time has passed—that I'm seventeen again, parked outside after youth group, afraid to go home because my own thoughts were louder than anything that awaited inside.

I stare out at the shimmer of the streetlights on snow, the old tree-house standing alone against the impenetrable black of the woods beyond the parking lot, and try to make sense of the confusion in my heart.

I can't tell if nostalgia is the thing that draws me back here, or if it's just the memory of Brayden's hand over mine, the way it made everything feel safe for exactly three seconds before reality crashed back in. My own palm rests on the steering wheel, the impression of his touch zapped onto my skin like a lingering current. I flex my fingers, trying to remember who I used to be, and who I could maybe, possibly, become again.

If this were a Hallmark movie—and, God help me, half of Maple Ridge wishes it were—I'd be on the phone with Mabel right now, plotting a redemption arc and listing all the life lessons I've learned in the last seventy-two hours. But it's not a movie. Tonight, I don't feel like a hero. I feel like a specimen under a microscope. The diagnosis would read: chronic, incurable misfit. The recommended treatment: avoidance, served with a side of snark.

I rest my head against the steering wheel and let the heat blast on high, thawing both my ears and my hands, resisting the urge to just drive straight until I disappear into the mountains and don't stop until I hit Bozeman.

If I wait it out, maybe I'll come up with some cosmic an-swer, some epiphany that'll make the years of doubt and regret untangle into something neat and manageable. Maybe the hot air will bake the confusion out through the skin on my cheeks. Maybe God himself will smack me across the head with an answer. *All good things come to those who wait on the Lord...right?* But nothing happens. I just sit, allowing the radio's tune of "Baby it's Cold Out-side" by Sinatra and Dorothy Kirsten to blend with the rhythm of my breathing.

Somewhere just past the haze of exhaustion, I real-ize the simple truth: I can't stay. Whatever this is—this half-life of pageants and hymnals and Sunday morning side-eyes—was never built to last.

I stare up at the white steeple, glowing against the black, and I know that's Brayden's home. Even if he left once. Even if he spent time lost and came back stitched together with threads of grace and willpower. He found meaning here. Rooted himself in the same soil I clawed my way out of. I can see him in there, probably alone by now, tidying programs, thinking through the words he'll use to build hope in a roomful of people whose faith is both armor and target. I picture him brushing glitter off his sleeves and humming "Angels We Have Heard on High" to himself while the sanctuary echoes with a peace he's long since made with his own heart. I want to believe I could be a part of that, or even that I could bring myself to want it, but deep down I know it's not for me. There's a gulf between the person who would stay for the promise of forgiveness and the one who still hasn't learned how to ask for it in the first place.

The tears surprise me. They come all at once, hot and blurring, so sudden and embarrassing I almost laugh out loud. I brace my palms over the steering wheel, head bowed to hide the evidence, even though I'm the only witness left in this parking lot graveyard. The salt tastes the same as every regret I tried to rinse out of my life in med school and residency; it stings but it also tastes, weirdly, like relief.

I let myself sob for exactly forty-six seconds, counting each one with the precision of a surgeon timing a suture. In that time I see an entire future—Brayden's, not mine—in all its best- case glory: Brayden, beloved by the town, raising a family with someone who can bake from scratch and believes with their whole heart. A woman who knows how to wear a Sunday dress and who fits into this puzzle without worrying about every whisper behind her back. Not a doctor who can barely keep her head above water, who still flinches at the word forgive like it's a bad placed stitch. The vision hurts, but it also feels honest.

I wipe my eyes with the back of my sleeve, digging my knuckles in just to make sure no traitor tear escapes. I'm not cut out for this. I'm a surgical tool, not a pastor's wife. I understand now. I can mend wounds and diagnose heartbreaks on an EKG, but I'm never going to be the kind of glue that holds Grace Hollow together. Brayden, with his flannel shirts and pageants, is the authentic article. He saves people for a living, and every eye in this church— maybe the whole town, whether it judges or forgives, turns to him for the next right thing. That wasn't my path before I ran, and even if I wanted it now, I don't think my name's on the wait list.

A few more minutes and the tears dry. I run my fingers under my eyes, check the mirror, and nod to the wreck staring back. "Okay," I tell her. "That's enough sentimentality for one night." I put the Jeep in drive and head home, the wheels crunching across the ice, the radio now silent. At every turn I picture the future rushing up to meet me—Brayden's broad-shouldered certainty, his calm.

Next time I see him, I'm going to tell him that I'm leaving—going back to New York for good this time.

Just that. No drama, no trail of emotional breadcrumbs back to Maple Ridge. I will finish out the pageant (because the idea of quitting gives me stress hives, and also because Hannah and the tinsel-eating cherub deserve that much), but then I'll say my goodbyes. To Brayden. To everyone. I will do what I should have done years ago: leave on purpose, with both eyes open, and let the town fill in my absence however it likes.

Ten

I cicles dangle from the porch roof, sharp and glistening. I stand shivering on the icy walk outside Grace Hollow, staring at a steel ladder that looks every bit as dangerous as the task at hand. The wind plucks at the box of Christmas lights I'm clutching, scattering the strands in a hopeless tangle of green wire and static electricity.

Brayden steps out of the utility shed, an orange extension cord slung over one shoulder, singing "While You Were Sleeping"—soft, steady, and surprisingly on key. The sound drifts across the snow, warm against the cold air, and I freeze halfway to the car, startled by how good he actually sounds. I recognize the song, though I couldn't name the artist if my life depended on it. His hair's damp with sweat and melting snow, the beard dusted white, his nose red from the chill. Somehow, he manages to look both rugged and impossibly gentle at the same time—and I hate that I notice.

He grins when he sees me eyeing the ladder. "You handled a glue gun like a pro. Climbing this'll be nothing."

"I did two years of ER rotation in the Bronx," I protest, "and never once had to dangle from a roofline."

"Small-town living has its perks." He sets the base against the porch, making a show of checking the rungs for stability.

"We only have two ladder-related incidents a year, and I haven't even broken my wrist since 2019." He offers the cord with a flourish, like he's inviting me to join in the mischief.

"Remind me why we're doing this last minute...in the evening?" I ask, jamming my hands deep in my coat pockets. The lights are freezing cold, stiff as surgical tubing.

Brayden shrugs. "Pageant's tomorrow. 'Operation Bethlehem' needs curb appeal. Mabel's orders."

I grunt, but he's right. Mabel had called at 5:30 PM sharp to say if the church wasn't lit up 'like the Star of David herself,' she'd hold the whole project in suspension. Mabel does not mess around.

The ladder groans as Brayden climbs, moving with a carefulness that belies his height and size. "Hand up the end?" he calls.

I untangle a section of lights and pass it up, watching as his fingers work fast, wrapping the eaves with a kind of lazy expertise. He glances down every so often to check my progress, which is embarrassing because I am absolutely not an expert at this. At one point the strand knots around my wrist and I nearly dislocate a thumb trying to pull free. "You okay down there?" Brayden asks, grinning like he's in on a private joke.

"I'll have you know this is more complicated than an endotracheal intubation," I yell up to him, tugging at a stubborn tangle of bulbs. "Do they teach knot-tying in med school, or is that specialization just for surgeons?" he calls down.

"Only the showoffs. I'm more of a trauma scissors girl," I say, pulling at the tangle with probably too much aggression.

"Color me shocked," Brayden says, draping a string perfectly along the gutter. "You always did hate the fine print." He steps down a couple rungs, close enough that I can see the flecks of snow in his beard. "Hey, hand me the next strand?"

I pass it up. Our fingers brush in the transfer, static snapping between us. I pretend not to notice, but Brayden's lips twitch into a smile that says he definitely did.

He loops the strand over a hook, then asks, "Remember that Christmas when Mrs. Keane let the youth group decorate the whole church by ourselves?"

I do. I laugh, hard. "Oh boy. The blue garland year. We used every roll in the area. The altar looked like a Smurf blew up in there."

He winks. "I maintain that it was an inspired choice. The congregation just didn't have the vision."

"They definitely didn't have something," I say, shaking my head. "Maybe eyesight, after that mess. We had to wear sunglasses for a week just to recover."

Brayden's laugh bounces off the eaves and into the night. The sound is pure nostalgia, bringing back every late-night caroling run and unsupervised youth group dare. Even the porch could probably still pass a blacklight crime scene test for glitter after that disaster. The memory stirs me in a good way, like removing a bandage and finding skin actually healed underneath.

Brayden leans against the ladder, one hand on his hip, studying the angle of the lights. "You know, not a single year since then have they asked the youth group to take charge of décor," he says, mock solemn. "There's a lesson in there somewhere."

"Yeah," I snort, "never trust two teenagers unsupervised with a budget and permission from the pastor's secretary."

He grins sideways at me, the ladder wobbling. "Even if they did, we'd just mess it up for the fun of it. That's, like, our entire brand."

I shake my head, but I'm smiling now, breath visible in the cold. I untangle the last set of bulbs and, with a little more confidence, climb two steps up beside him—close enough to smell the clean sweat and faint pine from his coat. "Stand aside, Reverend," I say, "I've got the steady hands here."

Brayden laughs, bracing himself with both arms so I don't knock him right through the choir room window.

"This is what makes you special, Tess. Underneath all that New York hustle, you're just a practical Montana girl with zero patience for stupidity." He grins. "But don't tell Hannah. She thinks you're a delicate city lady now."

"Please," I mutter, clipping the lights beneath the gutter with surgical precision. "If I ever got delicate, Mabel would ship me to a convent in Siberia for retraining."

He makes a noise of agreement, then adds, "You had more backbone than the rest of us combined, even as a kid. Just not always for the right reasons."

For a second it's just the wind and the steady clack of plastic light-clips against the cold vinyl.

I try to play it cool, but his tone catches me off guard. It's not a joke—a rare thing for him, and for me. I look him in the eyes. "Is that a compliment or a warning?"

He smiles, but it's the soft kind. "Just...an observation."

The hush that settles is a good one, a shared breath between nostalgia and now. Grace Hollow glows with the dusky promise of December snow, and I can see our handiwork—just a few more feet and the whole porch will look like a Christmas card.

By the time we reach the last corner of the eaves, the sky's fully inked in and the stars are spitting cold sparks above our heads. The lights snake down to the porch outlet, and I'm perched up top, placing clips in place so they won't blow off during the next snow storm. Brayden's at the bottom, anchor and audience, keeping a hand steady on the ladder and a running commentary going, just to make sure I know how precarious this is.

"Would be a real shame if the ER doc suffered a mild concussion before the pageant," he says, eyes gleaming up at me. "Very embarrassing for Grace Hollow's reputation, but I'd also get to fill out the 'accidental injury' line on the insurance forms. *That* could be embarrassing."

"Just think of all the sympathy casseroles at the next potluck," I shout, refusing to be baited.

"I'd bring you one personally. But it'd be hospital jello," he quips.

"Sadist," I mutter, snapping a final clip on. Above me the wind rattles the icicles, sending a fine spray down my neck.

"Don't look up," Brayden calls, but he's seconds too late.

A chunk of snow launches off the roof and explodes against my shoulder, nearly knocking me off balance. My hands scramble, and I flatten myself to the ladder, heart pounding. Thank God for small-town farm kid reflexes.

My heart's beating so hard I can almost hear it echo off the steeple, but with his hand on my leg, I manage not to faint or curse like I'm still working nights in the Bronx.

"Are you alive?" he yells up.

Embarrased, I blink snow out of my eyes and nod. "Didn't expect a roof avalanche. Sorry for—" My voice breaks because I'm picturing my own obituary, and also because Brayden's looking up at me with a concern that seems to be something more.

I try to laugh it off, but my hands are shaking as I clamber back into position, fixing the last bulb in place. From below, Brayden steadies the ladder, his gaze never leaving me. Under the porch light, his expression has all the softness of years and none of the distance I expected. There's something so gentle in the way he holds the ladder—like he's not just worried I'll fall, but hoping I'll come down willingly.

I take a breath, then another, and realize there's only one reason my heart's hammering this hard, and it's not the altitude. "Hey," I call down, voice too loud enough to echo down Main Street, "I can handle it."

"You don't have to," Brayden says, so soft it threads straight through the wind.

I focus on the rung in front of me, on the mindless task of spacing every bulb exactly four inches apart, but my hands are clumsy now. The words in my chest press upward, wanting out—to warn him, maybe, or just to get it over with so I can stop pretending, even to myself, that this ever had a chance.

I twist the last cord, press it flat, and risk a glance below. Brayden smiles up at me, eyes bright, but I'm about to say it—the whole thing, the hard truth I've been choking down for days. *You and me, Brayden, it's impossible. I'm not made for the life you lead. You deserve someone who actually believes in hope and potlucks, not someone who's been running from herself for a decade.*

I inhale, lungs tight, but before I can begin, he says, so quietly I almost miss it, "You know, I never stopped thinking about that Christmas. The last one before everything changed."

I freeze, my hands glued to the ladder rung, and suddenly the world is thrown back thirteen years: midnight snow, three dumb kids on a "borrowed" tractor, one flask of peppermint schnapps, and the gleam of Brayden's under the star light when he leaned over—not quite kissing me, not quite daring. The memory is a snowglobe, shaken and swirling until you can't see if it's heaven or disaster inside. My breath sticks on the rung of the ladder, the wind biting at my neck.

"Brayden—" I start, but the word tangles in the cold.

He looks up, smile steady, the blue of his gaze is winter clear. "I think about it more than I should," he says, voice a rasp that blends with the wind. "I guess I always knew it was the turning point. For both of us."

My grip falters, and I lose track of the bulb spacing. "Brayden, that's ancient history. Prehistoric. We were idiots, you know that?"

"I know," he says, but there's a stubborn softness. "Still. Sometimes I wonder if we'd have done things differently, or if we were just...destined to make the same mess, no matter what." He's still holding the ladder, grounding it against my shaking, and I can't tell whether I want to scream or cry or just let go and fall all the way down. I reach for the next light clip but my glove snags, and suddenly the world spins—boots slide off, fingers flailing. The ladder shudders and my stomach drops with it, a sick, weightless moment before gravity yanks me.

Strong arms grab my waist, catch me with impossible timing. The collision is hard and warm and nothing like the fall I braced for. The wind's knocked out of me, but Brayden's laughter is right at my ear, threaded with adrenaline and relief.

"Told you I'd catch you," he says, not letting go.

I'm half-hanging over his shoulder in a tangled embrace, and the only thing louder than my heart is the ragged sound of us breathing, sharing the moment like a dare. His hands grip my lower back, anchoring me, and my head is so close to his that I could count every freckle above his left eyebrow.

For a second, neither of us moves. The cold is forgotten, the wind is nothing. There's just the warmth radiating between us, the twin shivers of adrenaline and memory. My fingers fist in his jacket, and our faces are so close that I can feel the gentle brush of his breath on my cheek. If I closed my eyes, I think time would turn itself inside out and drag us both back to that winter night, before misplaced trust, bad luck and the accident that changed our "destinies" forever.

But I don't close my eyes. Instead, I look straight at him, searching for the thing he's been carrying in his voice all evening, the thing I can't bring myself to name.

"You know," I whisper, "if you were any other guy, this would be super awkward."

Brayden grins, not moving a millimeter, arms still locked around me. "But I'm not any other guy," he murmurs, like he's confessing a best-kept secret.

I'm pressed up against him, boots dangling, and his eyes don't leave mine for even a breath. His thumb grazes the back of my coat as he holds me steady, but it's the look he gives that almost undoes me—a mix of mischief and something deeper, undeniable.

We're frozen there for what feels like a full minute. He's still grinning, but underneath is a kind of hope I haven't seen on anyone's face in a long, long time. I'm not sure which of us is more surprised by it, but I know that if I let myself, I could fall into this space—into him—but I don't. I don't let myself. I remember, all at once, why I climbed the ladder in the first place. Why I said yes to this pageant, to this memory-palooza of a December: I was supposed to tell him. Tell him I was leaving for good. That whatever he remembered, whatever flicker caught in his eyes and haunted him at night, was hopeless. That I was a tourist in his world, never built for Sunday mornings or casseroles, let alone a future stenciled in with the same brand of permanence that ran in his veins.

Yet, dangling here, midair and wrapped around him like this, I want to believe it could work. That we could work. All I'd have to do is revisit the past I've kept shoved down for years. *No, I'm too damaged, too cynical, too whatever—for someone whose job, literally, is to believe things can be fixed.*

Brayden still has his arms around me, not caring about the snow soaking through our sleeves or the way the ladder's half- tilted behind us. I could say it now, the hard goodbye. I could push away, tell him about the importance of my job in New York, about "never meant to stay," about all the logical reasons I should let him walk away. Better to rip it off fast, one last act of mercy, my gift for this Christmas before everything returns to what it should be. I'd be gone in a week, anyway. That had been the plan since day one.

Except I can't do it. Not here, not when the world is ice and dark, not when everything inside me is suddenly a live wire desperate for connection. I want to stay in his arms and pretend, just for a heartbeat, that I belong. That I am not the sum of every mistake; that maybe, just maybe, the girl who left Maple Ridge could come home after all.

A long moment hangs between us, the kind that makes you aware of every nerve ending, every icy breath. I'm waiting for him to say something reckless, or for me to do something reckless, like close that last inch and dare the universe to smite us with a well-aimed icicle. Instead, we both just hold on, suspended, not quite in the past and not quite in the future, just two people and one almost-kiss dangling off the edge of a porch in the dark.

The universe, which apparently runs on the schedule of old television sitcoms, intervenes right on cue. A car door slams in the distance. I hear footsteps on the walk. The heavy tread of boots, a throat cleared with the distinct authority of someone who's seen lawbreaking at thirty yards. The porch light hits a big, blocky silhouette: Carl Johnson, sheriff's badge glinting under his jacket, brows knitted even more severely than the night I crashed my mom's Buick after junior prom. He pauses on the bottom step, eyes flicking up at Brayden and me with all the understanding of a man deeply unimpressed by gravity-defying romance.

Brayden lowers me with a gentle steadiness, but doesn't quite let go. "Evening, Carl."

Carl's mustache bristles as he stares at us through a fog of frozen breath. "Evening," he grunts. "Didn't realize this was how the city folks decorated their churches," Carl deadpans. "Occupational hazard, or...?" His gaze lingers on the overlap of Brayden's hand against my hip, the scene frozen under a halo of porch light and snow. Then, barely suppressing a smile, he jerks his thumb over his shoulder toward the road. "You two might wanna wrap this up. Weather's turning. Sheriff's office just called in a blizzard warning—roads'll get slick before midnight. Wouldn't want to see Grace Hollow's brightest end up in the ditch."

A surge of mortification races up my spine, as Brayden gently slides me down the last two rungs and I stumble onto the porch, boots skidding in the snow. The sheriff's eyes cut a line from Brayden's arms (still loosely stationed around my waist) to the lights, then to my face, red-cheeked and raw with cold, and his lips twitch in what I suspect is his version of a Christmas smile.

The Sheriff's gaze hangs on us for a fraction too long. I wonder if he's taking mental notes for the small-town grapevine or if this is just what passes for entertainment in Maple Ridge these days. Eventually, he shakes his head, issuing a half-sigh that's really more of a low chuckle, and then turns to the steps with practiced authority.

"Y'all have a good night," he calls back, letting the words plow a neat furrow through the cold. "And maybe keep your feet on the ground, yeah?" With that, he tromps back down the walk, boots crunching rhythmically out of sight.

Was he laughing?

Brayden waits until the truck's taillights are gone before he exhales, slow and warm against the December air. "He's been waiting two decades to catch us doing something dumb," he says, finally letting his arms drop away. "He'll be telling that story until the next blizzard."

I'm still mortified, all the blood in my body rerouted straight to my face. "Congratulations, we just gave the sheriff a Christmas miracle," I mutter, peeling myself off Brayden with as much dignity as possible. He brushes the snow off my coat with broad, careful strokes, and for a second I want to just burrow into that warmth and never come out.

Instead, I recoil to a safe distance and start coiling the extension cord, pretending it's the most urgent task of my life.

Then—just as I'm considering how to flee the scene without losing the rest of my dignity—Carl's voice echoes up the walk one last time: "You kids stay out of trouble, y'hear?"

It's so perfectly on the nose it takes all my willpower not to launch the bundle of lights at Brayden's head and the huge stupid grin on his beautiful face.

Eleven

The blizzard hits faster than the weather app—or even Sheriff Carl—predicted, swallowing the world outside Grace Hollow in white-out fury. I'm in the church foyer with Brayden, fingers still stiff from helping him hang the last of the lights before the wind tore through and the power gave out. The storm screams against the windows, shaking the old glass in its frames. Inside, the only light comes from the harsh, narrow beams of emergency spotlights, casting stark pools of brightness in the dark and leaving the rest of the sanctuary in deep shadow. The church feels both smaller and larger all at once—like we've stepped into another world.

"I think we're trapped," I say, voice unnecessarily low. He's staring out through the frosted glass, his breath clouding the window with each exhale. In the hush, it's impossible not to remember every Christmas Eve stuck here as a kid, warding off boredom with whispered dares and off-brand cocoa. Only now there's no buffer of a dozen other teens or a pageant full of shepherds; just me, the Pastor, and the wind howling like a town's worth of secrets.

He checks the door, wrenches it open half an inch, and instantly the vestibule fills with a curtain of snow and a blast of cold air. "That's a good guess," he says, shoving it closed. "Sheriff's probably right about the roads. And I'm betting that half the houses in town just lost power, as well."

I pull my coat tighter and flop onto the wooden pew by the coat racks. "So what's the drill, Reverend? Emergency cots in the sanctuary? Start a sing-a-long to keep morale up?"

He sighs and slumps down beside me. "Honestly, I thought we'd be out of here before the worst of it hit. I have zero emergency plan for exiles in the foyer."

"You, Mr. Community Center himself? I call your bluff."

He shrugs, lips twisting. "I figured you'd be gone after tonight. Or—" He stops, something fraying at the edge of the sentence.

"Or what?" I ask, not letting him off the hook.

He squints at the door, as if somewhere outside in that mess is an answer. "Or, I don't know. Maybe you'd stick around..but not like this. Stuck with me in the church. Funny, huh?"

I pretend to study the ceiling, painted with patchwork of ancient leaks and last summer's water damage. "You know, I planned to leave tomorrow but..." I want to bite my tongue so I don't blurt out the rest, but instead I quietly add, "I was going to say goodbye, Brayden. For real, this time."

He gives a half-laugh, but it's forced. "So we're really locked in, huh?" He stands, acting as though he didn't hear that last part, refusing to make eye contact with me.

He parks himself a breath away, elbows on his knees, like every crisis in his life is on this pew, waiting for him to come clean. "Guess it's just us and grace, then. Pun intended."

For a second, neither of us says a word. I can feel him beside me, silent, his body language unreadable—eyes on the floor. I reach for something to break the tension, fingers searching my coat pockets for the wrapped peppermint candies Mabel always stashed in the lobby—but I come up empty, so I do what I do best. I talk before thinking.

"You used to love storms," I blurt. "Remember the snowpocalypse of sophomore year? You built that monster snow fort in the cemetery and charged people five bucks to "repent" before midnight or risk the afterlife as a footstool."

For once, Brayden doesn't laugh. He looks up at me, and I realize too late that I chose the wrong story.

"That was Wyatt that led that enterprise." He doesn't say it with anger, just a flatness that puts a buzz in my ear.

Even thirteen years later, the name lands between us like a loaded gun. My pulse skitters. I stuff my hands under my thighs to keep them from betraying anything, but it's too late—he's watching me, blue eyes sharp as scalpels.

"I remember," I say, wishing I never brought it up, because now there's nowhere to hide. The foyer is too small for everything left unsaid.

He turns toward me, resting his head against the wall, and in the strange yellow-green light he looks older and somehow more breakable than I remember. He nudges the laces of his boots with the toe of one shoe, frowning, and the hush between us thickens. The wind flattens itself against the glass, then lets up for a fleeting second, as if waiting on a confession.

I open my mouth to say something—anything that isn't about the name we just let into the room—but he's faster.

"I never told you what happened that night, Tess," Brayden says quietly. "Not all of it." His hands are balled together, the knuckles pale.

"I know what happened...I was there! Remember?" I blurt it out, louder than I mean to.

The words ricochet off the walls, bounce around the empty foyer with nowhere to land. But Brayden just sits there, hands twisted together, waiting. It's a stubbornness I used to love, and now it makes me want to hit something.

"Can we just...not?" I say. "It was years ago, Bray. It's not going to change a thing."

But I already know I've lost; he's got that pastor's look, equal parts gentle and relentless, the one that says, I've decided I'm going wait until you give in.

"What exactly do you want from me?" I snap, the words jagged and mean before I can soften them. "You want me to admit it was my fault? That I crushed everyone's lives and then ran away? I already know. I never forgot."

He blinks, startled—a flicker of old Tess, the one who could burn every bridge in two sentences flat—but he doesn't retreat. "That's not what I want at all," he says, voice steady. "I just..." His jaw clenches. "I need you to know you weren't the villain...or the only one hurt."

The words stick on my tongue. I don't want to hear this—not from him, not here, not when the storm has turned every surface to cold glass and my nerves are trembling raw underneath.

I lunge for the old defense. "You don't have to comfort me, Brayden. I'm not sixteen anymore," I snap. I don't recognize my own voice: sharp, brittle. "You want ab-solution? Here—I forgive you. I forgive everyone. Let's pretend it never happened."

He flinches, barely, and it makes me want to take it back. But I don't. I keep going, because I'm afraid if I stop, the grief underneath will just burst out and take me with it.

"You want the truth, Brayden?" My voice is ugly, even to me. "I relive that night every time I try to sleep. That dumb party, the ice, the damn tractor. The way every-thing was fine until it wasn't. You think I need reminding? I built my whole life on being the cautionary tale. I've never even had a drink since that night! I don't get to have regular regrets—mine are forensic, in full color, every hour of every day."

I stand, pacing a tight circle in the open space, voice ricocheting in the lobby and into the empty sanctuary. "Wyatt wouldn't be dead if we'd made better choices.

Things would be different if I had said something. You wouldn't have had to..." My voice cracks at the thought of Brayden drunk in Chicago, living on the streets. *Great...more to feel guilty about.*

He listens to me unravel the rest, not moving, his hands wringing invisible water from the space between his knees. When the words run out—when all that's left is me, panting, jaw clenched, vibrating with angry regret, and tears running down my face—he doesn't try to fill the silence. He waits, lets the wind moan for us, lets the green glow of the exit sign cast us both as ghosts in the ruins of a church lobby.

I expect him to tell me I'm being dramatic. Instead, he stands so quietly I don't realize he's crossed the floor until his hand rests, light as air, on my shoulder. The last time someone touched me like that, it was in a trauma bay and the nurse was trying to comfort me after coding out a teenager. This is gentler, more deliberate. He waits until I look at him.

"I already forgave us, Tess. A long time ago," he says, voice so soft it's almost lost beneath the wind's assault. "I just want you to forgive yourself."

I shake my head, hard enough to make the room tip sideways. "That's not how it works—"

He cuts me off, gentle but immovable. "It was never your burden to bear." The words land heavy, like a benediction or a verdict. He squeezes my shoulder once, firm. "You don't need to carry it anymore."

Before I can respond, there's a thunderous crack—like a cannon firing right through the window. A tree branch, hurling itself from the storm, slams dead center into the hallway window leading to the classrooms. The glass shatters, shards raining down across the floor and up the hallway. The cold barrels in at once, scattering church bulletins from the table at the halls entrance and sweeping out into the lobby.

"Holy—" I say, and for once, don't censor it. We're running before we know it, boots slapping on seventy years' worth of linoleum as we hurtle toward ground zero.

The hallway and lobby are a cyclone of noise and glass. Wind slams papers across the lobby; snow whips every corner; cold knifing along every seam of my coat.

I stare, in shock, at what's left of the window: a jagged, impossible hole framed with Christmassy construction paper, the edge rimed in snowflakes. The giant branch—more like half a tree—sprawls across the hallway floor, needles and clumps of bark scattered everywhere. Tiny bits of foam board from the Sunday School displays flutter in and out like sad confetti. For a second it's just noise, shock, the bite of the storm dragging itself into the one place that was supposed to be safe from it.

Then Brayden's moving, already scaling what's left of the classroom hallway, grabbing a folding table to barricade the main draft. I'm right behind him, and suddenly it's a disaster triage, the kind I know how to do: he lifts up the table, I gather up stray hymnals, and together we prop it over the lower half of the busted window. He's already in the zone, sleeves rolled up, hair wild. "We need to reinforce it—it'll never hold if the wind shifts," he says, barely glancing back, and I'm already moving, springing to the janitor's closet before the words have cooled.

I duck into the closet, wrestling a roll of duct tape and a stack of trash bags out of the mess, tossing them back down the hall to Brayden while the wind screams just feet away.

We work like we always did—no words, just the muscle memory of a thousand group projects and mischief making "team building" projects. Brayden stacks the tables, shoves them tight to the glass, and I feed him tape, for once trusting him to make the fix stick. Together, we drag over two heavy choir risers from the music room and wedge them in front of the makeshift barrier.

Suddenly, we both lunge to steady a riser before it topples, ending up with our faces just inches from each other. For a second, neither of us moves. My pulse thunders, but all I can think is: this is exactly like before. Every crisis, every dumb scheme, every winter night we should've ended up in urgent care but didn't. Like some part of us always knew how to work together—how to fit, even when the world outside was more chaos than comfort.

We stand there, held in the moment, snow swirling against the barricade in crazy, electric patterns. Brayden's forehead glistens with sweat, his eyes shining with adrenaline or maybe something else—something older and more impossible to patch up.

Hell of a time for a kiss. Stop it, Tess, you're just still emotional. I step aside, a jittering, grateful, panicky breath escaping as I do. "We should check if the other windows held," I say, through a laugh that's more survival instinct than humor.

Twelve

The world is a watercolor of shadows when the power dies for good; the church sanctuary was tumbling from hopeful twinkle to candlelit hush in one startled heartbeat. Brayden and I are alone in the pews, clutching a discovered box of tea lights and a pair of flashlights that barely light the area around us. The storm outside gnaws at the old stone, sending shudders and flurries through the cracks, but inside, the silence is airtight.

I kneel in the first pew, arranging the candles in the stubby holders Mabel left by the choir loft, half-heartedly pretending I'm practicing for the pageant's processional. Brayden stands at the altar, staring up at the stained glass where, now, the only light is a wild, living thing, jerking across the pews each time the wind changes its mind. His face is ghosted in golds and blues, the kind of accidental majesty that would make a believer out of even the most jaded prodigal.

When he turns, the candles catch in his eyes, not quite enough to burn away the words hanging between us. He's waiting for me to speak; I'm waiting for the universe to provide a better time, a better story, a better version of the truth than what I've carried since the night it all went wrong.

"So," he says, voice pitched for a sermon, "what happens now?"

I line up the last candle, breathing in the faint, soapy scent of decades of wax and old hymnals. "Now," I say, "we admit we're completely unprepared for an all-night vigil with no heat and zero cell service."

He almost smiles, but the concern on his face doesn't fade. "We used to dream about being snowed in at the church," he says. "Remember? Midnight snacks from the communion pantry. Ghost stories in the balcony, even though we swore we'd seen every ghost this place had to offer."

I do remember. But every ghost has a name, and one in particular I can't let be silent any longer.

I wipe my palms on my jeans, the words finally assembling into something like confession. "I never told you everything about that night," I begin, turning the sentence over like a thorn in my mouth. "I let you believe what you needed to. I should have told you everything. But I didn't, because I thought maybe it would ruin your life. Or my life. Or maybe I was just... scared." Brayden's attention sharpens in the gold-blue candlelight. "I know the story, Tess. We all do. It was an accident. It wasn't—"

"This isn't about the accident," I say, and hear my voice shake. "We thought we were being sly and you know how the rumors always had every detail off by at least a mile?" I force my eyes up to his. "nobody knew the actual truth. Not even you."

His voice is soft, measured. "Then tell me," he says, almost a whisper, and sits on the edge of the stage steps, hands dangling loose, leaving space for me. "I'm right here."

For a second, all I hear are the bones of the building—shifts and sighs, the wind talking to itself in the rafters. I head up the aisle, drop onto the carpeted step beside him, knees bent tight to my chest. The cold seeps up from the floor, but I barely notice. I'm too busy rearranging the memory until it fits inside my mouth.

"I was the one who left the barn unlocked that night. It was supposed to be a joke, a way for Wyatt to prank Carl Johnson's prize heifer before the cattleman's breakfast. But we'd been drinking, more than any of us admitted later, and it got out of hand." My throat clamps hard, tight and burning.

"Go ahead," he says, softly. "I knew that part."

Taking a deep breath, I continue. "What you didn't know...is that I told the cops it was all me. That I'd gotten the liquor, that I'd dared him to drive it, that I was the one who egged him on. They believed me." I don't look up; I can't. "I made it all sound so clear and—well, you know how the sheriff was. It was easier for him to write the report if the 'bad girl' took the blame." The words rattle out like marbles on a tile floor, loud in the hush. "I just didn't want you to lose your future, Brayden. My whole life people expected me to screw up, and you—" I glance at him, tears blurring the candlelight. "You were supposed to be the one who got out. You had a shot."

I stop there, trembling, and Brayden just listens, quiet and still, letting the air fill with what I could never say before. His hands stay open on his knees, not reaching for me but not folded in prayer or judgment, either. The only thing in his eyes is a gentleness so raw I almost can't stand to look at it.

I run a hand over my face, half-laugh and half-sob. "You know, everyone thought I was just acting out, another episode of 'Tess being Tess.' But I wasn't. I just didn't want them to take you with me. I thought maybe if I made myself the problem, they wouldn't come for you, too." I pause, letting the ache settle in my shoulders. "I knew the sheriff was gunning for one of us. And I knew he wanted it to be me." My head drops, voice shrinking into the warmth of my arms. "I didn't know it would cost so much. I thought I'd just... face the consequences, and you'd be free to do everything I never could."

For a long time, there's only the slow creak of the sanctuary swelling and settling, as if the whole place is a living thing, listening. When Brayden finally speaks, his words are husky with disbelief. "You got the acceptance letter to Columbia University that week. You'd already lined up everything. Why— "

"Because I never wanted it as much as they thought I did," I say. "Not really." I let the truth bloom out, ugly and beautiful in the dim light. "I was supposed to go. And I did...go, that is. But all I wanted, right then, was for things to stay how they were, right here, with you and Wyatt alive and none of us grown up yet. The scholarship—Columbia, the city, all of it—it never felt real. Not like home did. Not like you did."

The last bit escapes before I can corral it, and I see the way his face twists—shocked, then sad, then something deeper that I can't diagnose.

For a couple of seconds, he just stares at me, mouth poised in a wordless question. Finally, his hand drifts up, pushing through his hair, and he lets out a breath so shaky I can almost see it in the dark. "You carried that?" he asks. "For all these years, Tess? Alone?" His voice is soft, not the stunned shout or the furious disbelief I always expected, but something quieter—tender and broken at once. "All these years, I believed you left to escape this place. That you were too smart and wild to get stuck in our little orbit."

I can't hold the eye contact. My gaze flickers over the melting shapes of the candles, the warped shadows on the old lacquered floor.

He goes quiet, and I think maybe he's going to let the vault close with everything unresolved inside. But then I see — really see — the way his hands tremble a little, the uneven set to his shoulders. He's reassembling the memory for himself, turning the idea of us over and over until it comes up raw on the other side.

"The whole time you were gone," he says, "I built this story in my head where you left because I failed you. Because I didn't warn you, or stop Wyatt, or keep things together when it counted. I thought it was my fault, too." He then says softly, almost inaudibly, "That's why they never questioned me."

"They didn't want you," I say, quiet and even. "They needed a scapegoat...and I gave it to them."

He's shaking his head, not in disbelief but in the slow disbelief of seeing a well-set bone for the first time—straight, but forever changed underneath.

He leans back, head tipped toward the stained glass, as though he needs to look through the ceiling for a second. "After the funeral, I... well, you know how it went." His mouth twitches, not a smile, not a grimace. "I spent the next year making sure there were no rules left in the county I hadn't broken at least once. I told everyone I was taking time to mourn, but what I really did was get fired from two jobs, pick fights, and drink enough to make my liver hate me forever." He rubs at his face with both hands, voice lowering.

The regrets re-ignite behind my ribs. "I didn't leave because I wanted to," I say, the old pain as bright as the day it seared me. "I left because I thought it was the only way to... rebuild something for my parents...and for you."

"I just wish you could've seen yourself the way I did," Brayden says, a hush in his voice that makes the shadows seem to listen harder. "Even then, Tess, you were the strongest person I knew. You always took the hit and didn't flinch, even when you should've. The rest of us... we just learned to hide behind you."

He stands and paces three steps, his silhouette stark against the flickering altar, then turns back. For a second I think he might try to make a joke of it, but his face is open, stripped of any shield.

"When you left," he continues, "I tried to find meaning somewhere else," he says, and his voice breaks on the word meaning. "I tried the city, just like you did. Nights got longer, mornings shrank—it was all noise and neon and nothing. I disintegrated for a while, spent some time on couches and in places nobody brags about. Until I ended up at that soup kitchen line at Pacific Garden which was not exactly my dream destination." He lets out a breath that's half a laugh, half a sigh. "You want to know irony?" he asks, hands braced on his knees. "Tom...the man I told you about the other day, was a second year Moody Bible dropout who pulled me into his prayer meeting by bribing me with vending machine snacks. But it worked."

He looks at me, eyes reflecting all the candlelight in the world, and the silence between us is loaded—more electric than awkward now, because there's nothing left to hide behind.

"After giving my heart to Christ, I stayed at the mission for a while," he continues, voice steady now, "helped out in the kitchen, swept the floors, listened to guys talk about hope like it was something you could find under a park bench.

He told me about Moody, too. How he'd dropped out after his own struggles with alcohol. The mission was his way back to something real—helping other broken people because of what he learned on his own journey back to God. He took me under his wing, and somehow, when I finally decided to apply, I had him in my corner, helping me fill out all the paperwork and telling me what to do. Other than good grades in high school, I got in because Tom believed in me...and because they believed that a broken young man could be someone God could use for great things." He gives me a sideways smile, sheepish and fragile. "In the end, Tom never finished his own degree, but he helped me get mine."

I listen, for what feels like most of the night, wrapped in his voice, as he tells his story, and for the first time in years I want nothing more than to lay down the armor I've been covering myself with since high school and just let him see me.

Brayden sits at the edge of the stage, hands folded, chin resting there, and the light turns him into a living statue: clear-eyed, battered, sincere. He seems as fragile as the candles that have mostly burned out, but I know the truth—he's become someone who now bends without breaking, whose faith is the thing that saves people with love and patience, not rules to control them. He is the same Brayden who once dared me to scale the gym wall during a youth lock-in, only now his dare is to trust again

I want to reach out, to touch his hand or his shoulder, something to anchor us in the same moment. Instead I just watch, memorizing the flicker of his smile as if it's the only source of light for miles.

He seems to read my mind. "You know," he murmurs, "it wasn't all your fault, what happened with Wyatt, you know? There's more to the story."

I open my mouth to protest, but he cuts in gentle as ever. "Wyatt's mom called me one night a couple years ago," Brayden says, voice so soft it nearly disappears under the howl of the storm. "Out of nowhere. She was out in Idaho, tending bar. I think she just wanted to hear a voice from before everything broke." He closes his eyes for a second. "She told me what the sheriff hadn't included in his initial report. That he left a note that night."

My breath lodges somewhere above my heart, refusing to move. "A note?" I echo, every cell in my body bracing for the impact.

Brayden nods, slowly. "She didn't show anyone, not even the cops, not right away. It was tucked in the glove box of Wyatt's mom's pickup, right with all the insurance card. She found it when she got pulled over that spring." Brayden's voice grows even softer, more reverent. "It wasn't long, and it wasn't full of explanations."—here his voice wobbles—" Sorry, Mom. I don't want to let anyone down anymore."

I can't speak. The words claw at my throat—rage, relief, confusion—but nothing comes out.

Brayden lets the silence spin for a minute, then brings his hands together in a quiet prayer steeple. "I used to think—" he starts, and then half-laughs, "I used to think that if I could crack open every second of that night, examine it like a forensic scientist, I'd find a way to fix it. I wanted to rewrite it so Wyatt didn't get on that tractor. So none of us ended up carrying ashes instead of memories." He glances at me, blue eyes lit with something fierce and unguarded. "Turns out, sometimes there's nothing to fix. Sometimes you just... have to trust God, and forgive everything else, like He would." His voice grows rough. "Even yourself."

We just sit there, leaning shoulder to shoulder, as if the only way to brace ourselves is to hold together. The candles drip unevenly, shadows blurring into the old knotty wood. Neither of us tries to push away the memory, or the grief. It's a new kind of peace, not pretty but real.

Maybe this was the closure I needed.

Thirteen

T he next morning I wake in the dark, disoriented, the pew's wooden edge biting into my ribcage. For several seconds, I mistake the low candlelight for the ER's trauma bay—the hush after a code blue when no one can quite say if the outcome was a win or a loss. But then the stained glass swims back into focus, casting a wavery map of reds and blues onto the walls of the sanctuary. I exhale, and the breath rises slowly, visible, warm.

Brayden is slumped on the steps of the altar, head tipped back, mouth open in the posture of a man who hasn't yet decided if he'll face the day or play dead a little longer. Soft amber halos bleed across his shoulders, and for the first time in forever, he looks like someone at peace—even if it's just because sleep found him after a night's worth of emotional heavy lifting.

I roll off the pew, crack my shoulder, and try not to think about how I must look after a night marinated in angst and candle smoke. Someone's scrawled "Merry Christmas Pastor!" in red marker on the pulpit whiteboard, which I definitely don't remember seeing last night. There's also a suspiciously empty tray that used to contain all of the sanctuary's communion wafers and at least three packages of leftover cookies, leaving only a dusting of crackers behind.

I gather my things—there's hardly anything, just my jacket, a dead phone, a half pack of tissues with every other one balled up from last night. Brayden's still knocked out, but when I step into the aisle, he stirs. A lazy, half-lidded squint. "Morning," he mumbles, voice like gravel and honey.

"Morning," I say, managing a smile that, against all odds, isn't fake.

He sits up straight, stretching until his back cracks loud enough to startle a literal choir mouse in the back of the sanctuary. I resist the urge to make a joke about it, mostly because I'm not sure my face can handle another round of ugly- cry right now.

Brayden pulls his jacket on, wincing as he rotates one shoulder. "If you're planning on sneaking out, you might want to reconsider." He gestures at the window above the side door. "You seen the drifts?"

I look. The snow is up to the lower stained glass—it's hard to even see where the churchyard ends and the world begins. For a heartbeat, all I can do is stand there and marvel—the landscape has gone arctic.

The graveyard is just ghostly humps and the steps out front are lost under a cartoon avalanche. Even our vehicles are almost gone—just the top of my Jeep Wrangler peeking above the furthest drift across—what used to be—the parking lot. The rest of Maple Ridge has vanished under a rumpled blanket of white.

As we take it in, a mechanical rumble breaks the silence. The sound comes from the end of Main Street—a pair of snowplows lurching through the storm wake, scattering snow drifts and shuddering against the curb. I watch in disbelief as Sheriff Carl's pickup pulls past them, hazard lights spinning like on a disco ball, just above the packed snow. The sheriff is living for this moment, you can feel it: the king of small-town crisis, first responder to every mailbox collision and lost dog.

Brayden pulls on his boots, nods toward the lobby. "Come on. If we don't get out there, he's going to send a rescue party."

We brave the chill and push open the front door, which only yields after a few concerted shoves. The outside air is a white roar, stinging my cheeks and blasting any residual sleep from my body. I stomp down the steps, boots immediately vanishing up past my ankles and to my knees.

It's still coming down, but lighter, the snow swirling in sheets over the fields. Sheriff Carl is already out of his truck, jacket zipped to his chin and a world-weariness in his gait that says he's done ten such rescues before breakfast. He gives us a chin- lift, then turns to the small gathering forming in the plowed-out hollow next to the church: a group of hardy locals, one guy in pajamas under a Carhartt, and—oh, God—my mother, in a coat with the hood trimmed in what looks like arctic fox.

She's trailed by Mabel, wrapped head to toe in layers that make her look ready for an Arctic expedition.

My brain is still rebooting from the vigil with Brayden, but right now, all systems are forced online by the oncoming embarrassment of facing half the town while wearing yesterday's makeup and someone else's sense of direction. I square my shoulders, breathe in the nose-hair-singeing cold, and nearly walk straight into my mother's outstretched arms.

Mom's hug is tight as a seatbelt, and instantly I'm seven again, bundled and fussed over, my face mashed into the faux-fur collar. Looking over her shoulder, I see Dad, bundled in his wool peacoat and that battered plaid scarf I bought at Walgreens in junior high.

There's a tightness around his mouth as he clocks me and Brayden together on the steps, but he covers it with a cough and a too-loud, "You two survive the night?" Like it's an actual question.

Brayden nods. "Church is still standing, thanks to some top-notch teamwork." He jerks his head at me, like I personally held back the howling winds.

Dad puts a hand on my shoulder, gentle but not patronizing, and I see the relief flicker across his face before he remembers he's supposed to be a stoic Montanan patriarch.

Mom holds me at arm's length and studies the circles under my eyes, the way my hair sticks out from my hat. "Did you even sleep?" she whispers, already dusting off the front of my coat. I shoot a look at Brayden, who is already mid-conference with the sheriff and a couple of the locals. They cluster around the tailgate, voices low but unmistakably pointed in our direction.

Mabel somehow totters up with her cane in this snow, gaze sharp and sparkling in the winter light. "Had us all worried, child," she says, but behind it is a grin that tells me the entire prayer chain knew exactly where I spent the night. "We were about to form a search party, but Carl here told us you'd be fine as long as you stayed at the church, where he last saw you. Looks like you outlasted the blizzard just fine," she adds, elbowing me in solidarity.

"There's pie at the house, when you thaw out."

"Thanks, Mabel," I say, feeling the warmth crawl back into my face in spite of the biting cold.

Brayden rejoins, dusting off his jeans (and somehow managing to look fresh despite the night camping in the pews). "Looks like Sheriff Johnson is calling a town meeting in the parking lot," he says, under his breath. "Is it possible to die of secondhand embarrassment?"

"Only if you let them see you flinch," I reply. I can't help but notice the way people glance away when I catch their eyes.

We shuffle over toward the tailgate gathering, the snow crackling underfoot. As Brayden and I approach, a circuit of looks passes through the group—fast, almost polite, but undeniably curious. I get a sense of headlines being written in real time: Two "trapped" grownups with a scandalous history, snowed in overnight at the church. In a town like Maple Ridge, that's front-page news.

The first person to break orbit is, naturally, Nancy Miller. She's got her lips triple-glossed and her phone out, probably updating the church page's "Prayer Chain" as she moves. She sidesteps the plow heap, plants herself at the edge of the group, and gives me a smile that is at least half teeth. "Looks like the storm didn't do half as much damage as we feared!" she chirps, the words pointed in the direction of the small gathering. "Thank goodness you both are safe." Nancy's jaw flexes with disappointment that no one had to perform mouth-to-mouth resuscitation, or at least that we didn't get eaten by wolves.

There are more than a few sidelong glances as Brayden and I shuffle into the circle. My dad stands a little taller, as if to buffer me from the rubberneckers. Mom threads her arm through mine, her grip iron beneath the fleece.

The sheriff clears his throat. "Folks, once the roads get a little more plowed, we'll get everyone headed home." He talks in a slow, practiced way, like he's emceeing a snowman pageant instead of directing a disaster response—discounting the fact that they all managed to arrive here in these conditions in the first place. There's a muffled chorus of agreement. The words "safety," "staying put," and "not doing anything foolish" carry the most emphasis. Half the crowd is still in pajamas, and one man is, I swear, holding a thermos full of eggnog.

But the real spectacle isn't the plan to dig out the town—it's me and Brayden, side-by-side in a picture so painfully Norman Rockwell that I want to crawl into a snowbank.

I tuck my chin deeper into my collar and risk a look at Brayden. He's got his shoulders back, his jaw set in a way I recognize means "brace for impact." For the briefest moment, I hate that I care about what these people think.

After all this time, my first instinct is still to dodge the blast radius of small-town judgment.

But then a different feeling floats up inside me—lighter, almost weightless. It isn't defiance exactly. It's more like resignation, mixed with this weird, exhausted courage. Because after a night spent digging up all the old wounds, I realize that I haven't been on this journey alone.

Brayden and I don't have to say a word. The simple physics of presence does the work for us—two exiles standing together, not flinching, not apologizing. The town will chew on that for a while, maybe a lifetime. I feel the eyes skittering off and on us, the way every old ache and rumor churns through the crowd, almost visible in the breath that hovers above their heads like dialogue bubbles waiting for captions.

A few paces away, Nancy draws a crowd without even trying. As if on cue, she links arms with Emily-in-Beige and whispers with all the fake discretion of someone hoping for me to over- hear, "I just hope things don't get complicated again, for his sake." She flicks her eyes toward Brayden as if he's a rescue puppy who might relapse at any moment.

I brace for the verbal attack, but then Mom's arm tightens around mine, and Mabel leans in with her head on my shoulder.

Dad strides forward, his posture tense as if he's ready to defend my honor himself. But before he can advance any further, Brayden reaches out and places a firm hand on Dad's shoulder, halting him in his tracks.

With a confident smirk playing on his lips, Brayden glances at us and declares, "It's time to put this to rest."

In one swift motion, he leaps onto the back of the Sheriff's tailgate, spinning around to face the crowd that has begun to murmur in anticipation.

Brayden clears his throat, and the hush is so stark you could hear a wish from a mile away. The wind drags at his jacket, snaps the corners of his shirt, but he stands easy—like he's always belonged on a makeshift altar, even if this one's a tailgate of a battered Ford instead of the pulpit of Grace Hollow.

"Morning, everyone," he says, and the voice is familiar but different—Brayden-the-pastor, somewhere between neighbor and big brother and the only guy who'll pray for you at two in the morning without making it weird. "I know a lot of you were up all night, and probably worried about something much bigger than the weather. I want to thank the sheriff, and every person who braved the roads last night to check on neighbors and family." He nods at Carl, who gives a solemn tip of his hat, then at the worn-out crew of locals, who smile in spite of the cold.

"But I also know," Brayden continues, "some people are struggling with more than snow right now." His voice is crisp and calm, the kind of tone that could talk a squirrel out of a tree, or a whole frozen town off a ledge. "And I've seen—over and over—the way this community can come together in times of crisis."

The crowd relaxes, small, awkward smiles flickering to life in the cold. I see Nancy's lips thin, as if she's not sure if she's being congratulated or called out. "But since the whole town is here," Brayden continues, "I can't help but feel a little extra responsibility to mention something that's been weighing on all of us, especially during a season like this."

He pauses, and I realize my lungs are holding back the air, waiting for the next words. "I don't think it's a secret that small towns have long memories," he says, his eyes sweeping the parking lot, meeting face after face, steady and without apology. "Even when we try to forgive, sometimes we end up holding onto things so tight we can't let in anything new. I know—" and here, he glances right at me, "—I've done that, too. It's easy to be haunted by ghosts. But the Christmas story is about letting go of old grief and finding a way back to each other, even if it feels impossible."

He turns, gaze landing on everyone all at once, and it's like watching a curtain drop across the past. "I know there are some here still waiting for the next scandal, or the next thing to talk about over coffee. I get it. Honestly, sometimes it's easier to talk about each other than to talk to each other. But I want to remind you—remind all of us—why we're here this morning, and every Sunday, and especially every Christmas."

He pauses, breath plumes from his mouth in a cloud. He presses on, voice ringing out clear as a bell. "We're called to love our neighbor, not just tolerate them. We're called to forgive, even when forgiveness sticks in the throat. We're called to remember that grace isn't a rumor—it's something real, and it's for every single one of us, not just the ones who seem to have it all together."

The crowd is dead quiet. Brayden takes a breath, then continues in a more conversational tone. "If you know our story, you know this church...this town faced tragedy. You know about Wyatt, and what happened that winter. I can't tell the whole story for you, because I'm not the only survivor. We all lived through that pain. And for years, we've let it define who we are. We turned it into history, into gossip, into a reason to keep people out or to keep ourselves apart. But the God I serve—He doesn't want us stuck in the past. He wants us to move forward. He wants to heal us and make us whole. That's why we celebrate Christmas—it's the story of a second chance for everyone. Every. Single. One."

It's quiet enough I can hear the rattle of a thermos cap. Nancy and her friends are fidgeting, but Brayden's got the rest of the crowd. Even my mother, who is clutching my elbow hard enough to bruise.

Brayden's hands spread, palms open to the crowd, and for a second I see the flash of the old Brayden, the boy with the wrestler's courage and the winter-blue eyes, only now it's filtered through years of loss, hope and conviction. "We've all suffered," he says, "So...you all deserve to hear the truth of that fateful night. Not so we can judge all over again. Not so we can find a new target," he looks at me again. "But so we can finally find closure and forgiveness. Together."

The crowd starts to murmur again, wondering what this new information could hold, or suspecting the truth on their own.

Brayden's gaze is steady, searching the crowd without flinch- ing. "There's something you should know about that night— something most of you never heard, because it never made the paper or the rounds of rumor." He glances at me, fast and sharp, but then looks right back at the faces in the snow. "Wyatt didn't just have an accident. He made a choice. And his family kept that heartache private...and so did I...out of respect, and out of love."

The words drop into the snow like fire. There's a collective inhale, the crowd shrinking into itself. Even Nancy's jaw goes slack, her phone half-raised mid-update.

A silence drops so deep that even the snow tires seem to hush mid-squeal. Brayden doesn't flinch. "He left a note," he says, softer now. "He didn't want anyone to ever blame themselves. Not me, not Tess"—here, his eyes find mine, fierce and gentle and unafraid of the town's gaze—"and not a single one of you. And he tried—he tried so hard—right until he couldn't anymore. That's not something you lay at the feet of a single person, or a single moment."

The tightness in my chest is so sharp I have to swallow it down, it, but it's too late. The words hang there, exposed and burning. For a second, nobody moves. Not even the wind.

Then something inside me—just can't take the weight anymore. I feel it in the pit of my stomach, a surge of every memory I've spent the better part of my life trying to remove, or numb, or just plain outrun. The years of blaming myself, of biting my tongue and bracing for impact; the tired guilt that never really went away.

My jaw is clenched so tight my teeth ache, but still, I can barely breathe. *I can't do it.*

The muscles in my legs twitch, and before my mind can catch up to my body I'm already moving—pushing through the cluster of down coats and coffee breath and a thousand eyes zeroed in on me like I'm the only sinner left in the zip code. Every step is a micro-earthquake, but I keep going, past the tailgate, past the line of snow-muted pick-ups, until the world narrows into the hard blue cold and the loud hush of my own heartbeat.

Fourteen

I t's freezing in the sanctuary, the heat still not yet
having a chance to warm the open area, and still I
sit here in the front pew, shivering and searching for
whatever scraps of soul I haven't already offered up as
penance. It's too cold for someone to cry, but my eyes do
it anyway—hot, ridiculous tears running sideways down
my face and pooling in the hollows above my scarf. My
nose is running – I let it drip.

For what must be the millionth time in the past twen-
ty-four hours, I try to piece together the old story: three
kids, one flask of schnapps, and a borrowed tractor. It
used to be tragic in a way that belonged to everyone—a
shared tragedy, a cautionary tale you swap at sleepovers.
Now, I know the fine print. And it is so much worse. It's
not just Wyatt in the snow or the sirens through the

black, but the secret in the note, and every invisible ache he carried that I never even saw. All those years I thought I was the villain. Turns out, I was just a blind idiot.

The story keeps replaying itself—Wyatt's mom finding the letter, the spiral of pain it must have cost her. Brayden being told years later and shouldering the burden of that knowledge alone.

I bury my face in my hands and let the ugly crying go full throttle. There's no one here to see it—just me and Jesus on the stained glass, staring down with that infinite patience that makes me feel three feet tall. My shoulders hunch, my whole body folding in on itself, and the sound that ekes out is equal parts rage and grief. I want to throw something. I want to unwind every year I spent believing a lie so I could leap back in time and just...ask Wyatt what was wrong. See him, really see him, even once, before the story changed for good. *How did I not know?*

I was so loud about being the mess, about being the one who broke things, that I never bothered to see Wyatt at all. I blamed myself for the party, for the keys, for the tractor. "I'm responsible," was always my line, as if the world was a checklist and you could account for every variable if you just paid attention. But I never paid enough attention to see what Wyatt was actually carrying. I could rattle off his GPA, his shoe size, his favorite brand of energy drink, but not the darkness gathering behind his eyes.

I squeeze my eyes tight, as if the world would stop existing if I just refused to see it for a minute. *God, is this how you wanted it?* "Do you even care?" The words are out before I can catch them, bitter and fast.

"If He does, then why does He let pain pile up like this?"

Dad. His voice echoes through the cavernous sanctuary, slow and measured in a way that's meant to offer understanding and to prod me into thinking harder at the same time.

He doesn't come any closer at first, just stands in the main aisle, shoulders squared under the weight of his old wool coat. I wipe my nose and whip around, startled, not only because I didn't hear him enter, but because I didn't expect him to be here at all.

He doesn't say anything else, doesn't even clear his throat, just lets the silence between us stretch until it's almost part of the structure, built into the beams and the cold echo of the room. There's the sound of his boots on the carpet, and then the warmth of his outline as he moves down the aisle, pausing at the end of the pew like a doctor waiting at the foot of a hospital bed.

He considers me for a long moment, and in that half-light I see all the years I've spent running away from his approval, his judgment, even his love.

He sits down beside me, his presence pulling me closer, like gravity itself is conspiring for comfort. He doesn't start with a speech or a platitude, just lays his hand on mine—his touch heavy, familiar, the way you brace a splint: steady, matter-of- fact, unafraid of the break beneath—a tenderness.

"Dad," I manage—trying to regain my composure.

He's an expert at waiting. He lets the cold sanctuary fill up with whatever needs to pass between us—sorrow, memory, the hush of unspoken questions. The set of his jaw is the same as when he'd patch up my knee after bike crashes—just put your hands on, do the job, and don't panic over the pain that leaks out.

My breath hitches, and I blurt, "It wasn't even what I thought. I spent all this time believing it was my fault—Wyatt, the night, the whole thing. But I didn't even see him, Dad. I never noticed he was hurting." I can't look at him; I'm half sure if I do, I'll lose the power of speech entirely.

He squeezes my fingers in his, thumb tracing the knuckles. "I know," he says, with a note of softness in his voice that I don't think I've ever heard.

I stare at my dad's face, retracing every year I spent convinced I was the single point of failure in our family's history, all the times his silence felt like a locked door. The words "I know" clang in my brain. *Did he know about the note the whole time? Did he keep that a secret, or did he mean something else entirely?*

I want to ask, but the question catches on the knot in my throat. Dad doesn't let go of my hand, not even when I try to pull away to wipe my face.

He clears his throat a little, and when he speaks, his voice is low and less clinical than I've ever heard. "You always were too hard on yourself, Tess," he says.

I brace for a lecture— maybe an anatomy of all my failures—but instead he just looks at me, really looks at me, like he's finally ready to see the adult person sitting beside him instead of the ornery teenager who once swiped his keys and crashed his car straight into the mailbox.

"I know you," he says again, gentler this time—adding "you" to complete the thought. "I mean it. Even when you were a little girl, you carried everything for everyone else. Like the world was going to drop if you stopped for a second." He lets out a long, slow breath, running his hand down his jaw. "You took the blame for everything. Sometimes you even tried to take the blame for things you couldn't control."

His voice goes softer, almost as if he's talking to himself. "I always thought that was the bravest part of you. I also always thought it was why you'd end up breaking before anyone else." He shakes his head, a smile in it somewhere despite the sadness. "I wish I'd told you sooner that you never had to carry all that alone."

"I know I wasn't easy," I say, voice croaky and thin.

He gives me a half-smile, the one he only ever used for broken bones and stubborn dogs. "You weren't supposed to be easy, Tess. Have you met our family?" He lets the question hang, almost a joke, but then he softens. "I always admired the way you pushed against everything. Even if it meant you and I butted heads from here to Bozeman and back. I figured you'd end up somewhere other than Montana, but I didn't count on how much it would hurt to watch you leave...or how much you would torture yourself in the process."

He looks up at the stained glass, the colored light catching in the wrinkles along his brow, and his eyes get that faraway look I remember from when he used to read me stories before bed.

"I always thought you were angry at me," I say, voice trembling so hard the last word gets lost. "Like, disappointed. Every time I did something wrong, I felt like I could see it in your face."

He doesn't answer for a second, just looks down at my hand in his. "That's on me," he says at last. "I never had words for any of it, what you were going through. Your mother could talk the sadness out of a dog in a ditch, but I never knew how," he admits. "You get your stubbornness from me, but your feelings—those were always your mother's department."

I press my lips together, not sure if I want to laugh or take offense. "Well...I felt like I always let you down," I say, and the accusation lands flat, small, but real. "Even when I tried to get it right."

He shakes his head, quick and emphatic. He gives me this look—equal parts wry affection and weariness. "Honestly, there were times I was disappointed. But usually I just never knew how to tell you I was proud without embarrassing you...or me." My throat goes tight, but there's a fragment of warmth in the middle of all the mess. "I even felt you were mad that I was home," I say. "Mom hugged me and told me how much she missed me, but...this is the most we've even spoken since I've been here."

He actually laughs, a soft bark that echoes against up the peak of the sanctuary. "Tess, if I could have you home every day, I'd take it, even with all the drama and broken fences and everything. But I didn't want to get used to you being here." His eyes glisten just a bit in the weird light, but he keeps it together. "Because I figured you'd be gone again, soon enough. You always had some place bigger to run to. I just wanted you to... find your way."

He releases my hand and leans forward, elbows on knees, gaze locked on the altar like it's holding up half the church.

He sits quiet for a time, then shifts his gaze sideways. "You know, you asked God a question a minute ago. Right before I sat down." He says it gently, but there's something behind it—a nudge, not a rebuke. "You said, 'Do you even care?'"

I blink, startled into embarrassment. "Yeah. Well. Seemed fair, considering."

He absorbs this without flinching, then ducks his head closer to my ear. "I've wondered the same plenty of times." He folds his big hands in his lap. "Probably more than you have before I stopped pretending I had the answers." He rubs his face, old guilt and new humility mixing into something open. "I'd drive out to the edge of town and sit on the tailgate, just...talking out loud to God, sometimes. Sometimes angry, sometimes just confused. And I'd always end up trying to bargain: please, fix my screw-ups. Please, keep her safe. Please, let her come home just once so I can say the right thing, this time." He shrugs, looking suddenly sheepish for a sixty-something doctor. "It never seemed to matter how stubborn I got. I prayed." He laughs. "And in all that, I finally came to a realization..."

He pauses then looks me in the eyes with a strange gentleness. "Is it that He doesn't care?" he asks, voice low. "Or...is it that we get so busy complaining about our own issues, that we never take the time to notice He has been right here all along...by our side this whole time?"

I start crying harder—dumb, but at least it makes sense now. I let myself lean against my father's solid shoulder, an anchor in the storm that is my soul.

Later in the day, Grace Hollow is a triage scene. Chunks of glass crunch in the entryway; folding chairs double as barricades; everywhere, the aftermath of the blizzard is tangled up with the aftermath of a hundred years' worth of Christmases. I'm running on three hours' sleep and the help a styrofoam coffee cup, but my head feels clearer than it has in years.

Word spread fast—small towns run on gossip, but they run even faster on group obligation. There's a crowd in the sanctuary that started forming just around the time my tears dried up: the men of the congregation staring at the downed tree in the hallway, saws in hand.

Their tools and voices rise and fall in a way that's almost musical; the rhythm of this town's muscle memory kicking in. My dad is down the hallway patching up a pane of glass in the shattered window, while Hannah and two teens sweep up the glittering mess on the hallway floor.

There's Mabel, clipboard in hand, orchestrating a re-sort of the pageant Christmas props like she's directing traffic at JFK. My mother presides over the kitchen, bossing around anyone within earshot, sustaining the entire clean-up operation on buckets of coffee and a running commentary about "acceptable work ethic." Every few minutes, a new volunteer arrives— someone with a snow shovel, a Shop-Vac, a pair of mismatched gloves and a can-do attitude. Some come with casseroles or cellophane-wrapped platters of fudge, others just with stories about the blizzard and a willingness to pitch in.

It's the one thing Maple Ridge does perfectly: collective, unspoken coordination in the face of a mess.

I duck into the main office, intending to find a first-aid kit for the handful of nicks and scrapes already starting to accumulate, and instead run into Brayden. I nearly bowl him over—he's on hands-and-knees in the supply closet, digging through years of clutter. His hair's wild, eyes bright with the full-throttle panic of a man tasked with making a shatter zone look like a house of God. There's a streak of what I think is blood on his cheekbone, but also possibly red Sharpie. Hard to tell, honestly.

I hold out my own little first-aid kit and shake it like a peace offering. "Need a triage nurse?" I ask, and the sight of my own, mostly-normal face in the safety glass makes me grin.

He sits back on his heels and grins up at me, as if he's genuinely shocked to see I haven't fled the building. "Doc Somerset, reporting for duty?" he jokes, then loses the thread of bravado as he sees me properly. "You okay?" His voice is a whisper, meant for just us.

The answer is, unexpectedly, yes. I'm more than okay. Something—maybe the talk with my father, maybe the sheer electricity of community at full tilt—has untangled the panic I was choking on since I've come home. There's still the entire history wedged between us like the world's ugliest bookmark, but yeah, I'm okay.

"Only if you include hazard pay for snark," I say, and toss him a box of band-aids. He peels one open, slaps it on without a wince, then tosses the wrapper over his shoulder with a grin. The office is small, but he makes space for me just the same—legs folded, gaze inviting.

"So," I say, settling on the floor next to him, knees touching as we sort through a chaos of packing tape, blue painter's tape, and what might be an unopened can of ravioli, "is there some kind of badge for disaster response, or do small-town pastors just get extra credit when the roof caves in?"

He cracks an exhausted smile. "There's a special sash for it. Complete with glitter glue, only allowed for true veterans." Then, gentler, "I mean it, Tess. You good?"

I nod, and this time I don't have to fake it. I'm still raw, but the edge is gone.

I lean my head back against the wall, listening to the laughter and saws, the clatter of brooms and the buzz of a dozen conversations all weaving together like a quilt. Out there, in the sanctuary and the hallways, there is a current of energy that feels—strangely—like hope. Maybe, in some weird way, this is what church was always supposed to be: people showing up for each other, patching the broken stuff, arguing over who gets the last of the real creamer, then laughing like none of it hurts. Someone in the hallway yells that the window is holding, and another volley of laughter carries down the corridor. Here in the office, Brayden and I are pressed side-by-side on the linoleum, hands lost in the deeps of a supply box that, by sheer stubbornness, refuses to yield a single roll of actual duct tape. Just as I'm about to abandon the search in favor of stapling the window shut with pure willpower, I hear footsteps—heavy and deliberate—then the familiar, awkward throat-clearing of my father in the doorway.

He looks at us, at the tangle of supplies and the glitter on Brayden's sleeve and the new, half-clumsy bandage on Brayden's cheek. For a second, I think he's going to launch into some kind of warning about bodily injury and insurance forms, but instead Dad just rests a palm on the door frame and gives us both a look—equal parts bewildered and proud.

"You two got a handle on this?" he asks, but it's not really a question. I realize, with a start, that I've never seen my dad quite so at ease around me and another person. He's usually the kind of man who hovers at the periphery, all wit and clinical detachment, but right now he's just...smiling. For no reason, except maybe this is the first time he's seen me like this since I was a teenager—tangled up in a mess but actually laughing in the middle of it.

Dad pulls a battered chair up to the doorway and sits backward on it, arms resting on the seat back. "We got another problem," he says, and he's got that glint in his eye that means it's not a real emergency, just something he wants to see if I can solve. "Heard you're light on volunteers for the pageant tonight. Hannah says the Joseph costume is three sizes too large for any of the volunteers."

Brayden blinks, surprised. "Oh. Yeah. The, uh...previous Joseph was out of town when the storm hit."

Dad, who has never volunteered for anything not directly involving first aid or the annual community blood drive, cocks his head at Brayden. "What's the backup plan?" he asks, as if there's a possibility the solution will be surgical in nature.

Brayden shrugs, toying with the roll of painter's tape. "Right now? If we can't convince somebody's dad to wear the robe and stand on stage, we're moving to Plan B: cardboard cutout of Joseph from last year's nativity. Hannah's already prepping the stand."

Dad gives a witty little smile, then glances at me, then at Brayden with a look that could out-sass a drill sergeant. "I'll be Joseph," Dad says, and the words are so uncharacteristic I nearly choke on my own spit. "Nobody will question my beard, and it's better than cardboard." He shrugs. "Besides, your mother says if I don't, she'll do it herself and bring shame to the entire Somerset clan."

Brayden actually claps, startling himself and me. For a second I wonder if I dreamed it, if maybe I hallucinated the whole moment, but the glint in my dad's eyes is too proud to be fake. He's still basking in the glow of being the pageant hero when Nancy Miller, patron saint of the passive-aggressive side-eye, glides past the open office door. She's got her phone in one hand and a sheet of pageant notes in the other, and when she spots me, her stride falters just enough to scan the room. The smile she pastes on is not her normal practiced one, but there's an extra note in it this time—almost a real one, the tiniest quiver of apology in the set of her mouth. For the first time maybe ever, Nancy looks at me and instead of the usual look that says "I will drag you before a church tribunal," she delivers something almost resembling re-spect. Or surrender. Or—it kills me to admit—a truce.

She doesn't utter a word; just wags the pageant notes, gives me a nod and a close-lipped smile meant for no one else, and continues down the hall as if running out of pa-tience would break her contract as head town busybody. I nearly laugh. If that isn't a peace offering, I'm not a doctor.

After Dad leaves to find Hannah, Brayden and I are still side- by-side on the ugly blue tile, our knees pressed so close together they might be taking vows.

We actually sit there for a long minute, anchored to the floor by the chaos and our exhaustion and the weird, electric thing that happens when you realize you are no longer the person who ran away. For once I'm not thinking about leaving town, or what I'll say to Brayden, or whether my dad is going to hug me or just shake my hand at the airport. It's just...here. Today. The church, the clean-up, the sun shining off the fresh snow outside and the sheer relief of not being the punchline to every story in town.

Brayden nudges my knee with his. "You know," he says, "God certainly has a way of bringing people together."

Fifteen

Nothing says "redemption" like a nativity pageant starring three sheep in snow boots and a Mary who is, at this moment, eating a granola bar behind the manger. The sanctuary is packed; kids with pipe-cleaner halos jostle for a glimpse of their parents, and every adult in town is a shade of radiant, sleep-deprived, or slightly mortified. The coffee in the foyer has been refilled twice. Every pew is crammed with puffy parkas, and the heating has finally, blessedly, caught up. Grace Hollow is alive with the kind of anticipation you usually only find at county fair bake-offs or the state wrestling finals.

Backstage—or rather, behind the creaking velvet curtain that Hannah swears is "authentic, not just old"—the small cast huddles in tangled tinsel and last-minute nerves. My job, as the only adult under the age of forty-five who can both herd children and charm a mal-functioning sound system, is to keep the peace and the pageant moving. I am not, as previously threatened by Nancy Miller, actually in the show. That honor goes to the next generation of local prodigies, plus a few freshly-recruited stand- ins for the shepherds and wisemen (thank you, Brayden, for guilt-convincing three high schoolers who would rather have been at the gas station parking lot eating Fritos).

The lights dim without warning and Brayden takes the stage, miraculously looking neither frazzled nor sleep-deprived, which is a minor Christmas miracle in itself. He's swapped the plaid for a solid-color dress shirt—blue, a good choice—and he stands at the pulpit with a calm that could only be practiced before a mirror, or perhaps in the aftermath of a five-bell trauma. The kids fall instantly silent; even Ben, who spent intermission demonstrating how to weaponize a halo, starts behaving as if Gabriel himself is watching.

"Welcome, everyone, and Merry Christmas," Brayden says, and his voice pours over the crowd like something warm and carefully applied. Not syrupy, not even particularly pious—just simple, and good. "If you're here this Christmas Eve, you're family, and if you're family, tonight is for you."

There's a hush, the crowd collectively leaning forward. My pulse skips. I peek past the curtain as Brayden lays out the Christmas story. He's got the room in the palm of his hand, even the most cynical, even the "Chreasters" who only show up twice a year. The words aren't the ancient, rote ones; he makes them new, each syllable spun out like it might save a life.

"Good evening, dear friends," he says. "Tonight, we gather to celebrate the birth of Christ through a special pageant. As we watch Mary and Joseph's journey, the angels' song, and the shepherds' awe, let this story of love and redemption in a humble manger renew our hope and faith. Let's open our hearts to the light of our Savior's birth."

Brayden steps aside, and the spotlight finds Lainey—a high school sophomore with a strong voice and steady nerves that would make a trauma surgeon proud. She stands front and center in a dress borrowed from her older sister and sings "O Holy Night" with a shaky courage that gets braver with every note. Somewhere in the back, her mom is openly sobbing, and even her rugged father has to hide his grin behind his hand.

I stand in the wings, heart hammering a little too fast, watching the stage through a slit in the curtain as Lainey's song builds and builds, causing my arms to break out in "goosebumps". Moms dab their eyes in the third row; dads clear their throats. The kids feeding lines from the wings are suddenly hushed, looking holy in their bathrobe costumes and bent coat hangers. The crescendo hits, and for just a second, the world feels softer.

I can see Brayden, the steady set of his shoulders, his face drinking in every word. My own heart is an electric reminder of how much has changed over the course of the past few weeks. For all my determination to leave, to pack up my unresolved history and vanish back into the noise of New York, I find myself rooted here, unable to move—not wanting to move.

The tingling in my hands isn't from the soundboard wiring or the stress of wrangling children for ninety minutes—it's the kind of nervous, bright energy you only get when you're exactly where you're supposed to be, but too scared to admit it. I flatten my palm over my chest like I can steady my heart with pressure. It doesn't work. Instead, I flash back to the way Brayden's hand curled around mine in the church basement and then the warmth of his presence last night in the sanctuary during our terrible, beautiful time together.

I can still feel the press of his knee against mine in the cramped closet, the warmth radiating through jeans, and the words that Brayden spoke hanging in the air between us. The words loops in my mind like a carol I can't stop humming. *Did God really bring us back together?*

The house lights go down, and suddenly the pageant is in swing. Sheep trip up the steps; the "innkeeper" (played by Ben, seven, future lawyer judging by the cross-armed authority) refuses Joseph at the inn with such force that it nearly becomes a wrestling match. Mary, chewing gum with regal indifference, produces a baby doll Jesus in a moment so deadpan it deserves an Emmy.

During the overture of cardboard sheep and makeshift stars, Brayden's gaze finds mine through the seams in the curtain as he returns to the stage, and for a single electric second, the years between us collapse. We're seventeen again, side-eyeing each other from across the gym, telegraphing whole conversations with a raised brow or the tiniest tilt of the mouth. My pulse jumps in my throat, and I duck back behind the curtain, mortified at how much I want to be caught by his eyes again.

Brayden is front and center, narrating the nativity through a lens that is both timeworn and totally brand new. He tells the story in quick, vivid cuts: the panic of Joseph's journey, the stubborn love of Mary, the chorus of angels in the high. He's not reading, not phoning it in—he's mining it out of memory, like each word is a piece of himself. The whole room is with him. Even Nancy's prayer-crew looks like they're feeling things they did not sign up for.

I'm still riding the adrenaline high when it happens—the show-stopper, the one moment that every parent dreads and every child actor has nightmares about.

Second Angel—Lilly, age six, crowned in wire and glitter— strides onstage for her single line, steps up to the mic, and blinks hard at the rows of adults and iPhones staring her down. She opens her mouth and nothing comes out. Dead air, heavy and endless. The pause stretches. My own hands start to sweat.

From the wings I try the universal "stage mom" charade— mouthing the first words, giving the most exaggerated nod in the history of Christmas productions.

Lilly looks to her left, then to her right, and I can see the wobble start in her chin, the first ripple of imminent meltdown. The whole sanctuary leans forward as one, unconsciously bracing for the shipwreck. I remember what Brayden said about grace being for people who already know they'll never measure up, and suddenly I'm on my feet and onto the stage before my brain can veto the decision.

The floor is covered with hay. I kneel next to Lilly, balancing on my toes so my face is even with hers, and I whisper, "You've got this, kiddo," and she looks up at me, blue eyes brimming.

Her lips are trembling. "I forgot," she whispers, and the entire crowd hears it, as if her anxiety is broadcast directly into the town's soul.

Every thought I ever had about being alone bubbles to the surface in this moment. So I squeeze Lilly's tiny hand, lean my mouth to the oversized mic, and rescue us both: "Sometimes angels forget what to say—and that's okay, because the best messages come from the heart anyway. Want to try together?" She nods, and her hand clutches mine like a lifeline. I speak softly into the mic, eyes on her and not the buzzing audience. "What do angels always say first, Lilly?"

She thinks hard, brows scrunched, then manages, "Don't be afraid?" It's more a question than an answer, but her voice is clear, ringing over the hay and the crowd and the bright whiteness of the stage lights.

"Exactly," I say, and squeeze her hand again. "Don't be afraid," I repeat for the congregation, and it echoes out into the church, past the garlands and the stained glass and every face that ever braced for disaster and I help her take a deep breath and say, "Fear not. For behold, I bring you good news of great joy, which shall be for all people."

The words echo through the sanctuary—big, ancient magic— and Lilly's voice, barely above a whisper, finds its shape. "For unto you is born this day in the city of David, a Savior, who is Christ the Lord."

Her face lights up. The audience exhales and someone— probably Mabel—lets out a ragged sob in the amen corner.

There's a fevered beat of applause, more for the courage than the delivery, and Lilly's posture squares itself into shape. She blinks at me, then at the audience, then at Brayden—who gives her an exaggerated thumbs up—and the trembling leaves her hands.

The sancturary is so quiet that for a moment you can hear only the creak of snow melting off the roof, the faint hum of the sound board struggling to keep up. Out there in the pews, every parent with a nervous kid on stage is blinking away tears, and every prodigal—myself included—feels the tangled knot in their chest loosen, just a little

Something happens as I stand there, looking out at the rows of faces lit with candle-glow and hope. The air in the church shifts—like all the years between me and this place dissolve, and every secret, every old regret, gets folded into something new and bearable. I kneel by the kids for the last chorus, helping them mouth the words. I catch my dad's proud, stoic grimace in the third row, and even Nancy's frozen expression as she registers the parallel (me, the prodigal) and tries to decide whether to clap or weep.

We step back together, as if neither of us wants to let go, and the next angel enters with a confidence borrowed from Lilly's small victory.

Brayden stands just behind the curtain, his eyes on me. In that flicker of a second, I see something I've never let myself acknowledge—pride, yes, but also faith. Not faith in the situation or the pageant itself, but in me. It lands, a full-body jolt, heavier than every regret I've ever carried. In the breathless hush after Lilly's line, I understand: I am exactly where I need to be. Not because I'm fixed, or because Maple Ridge has unspooled all my tangled history, but because my whole weird scramble of a journey has led to this one ridiculous moment where I stop running and just... exist.

The final chorus, "Silent Night," is less a performance and more a communion. Kids, parents, half the church join in, and somewhere between the off-tune harmony, I'm hit with the kind of tidal emotion that makes you want to both laugh and ugly-cry at the same time. The walls, battered by years of history and at least two blizzards, seem to breathe out all the old stuff and make room for this new, bright ache.

Afterward, my mom finds me first, arms already open, her eyes shining brighter than any of the string lights jury-rigged along the ceiling. She wraps me in a velvet-fisted hug and cups my cheeks like I'm still twelve, whispering, "You did so good, honey," over and over with a kindness that is almost unbearable. Dad's right behind her; he waits his turn, then pulls me in with a gentleness usually reserved for the very young or the very broken.

His beard smells like coffee and a trace of plastic table-cloths. He holds me close, murmuring something about how proud he is like it's hardwired to trip out of his mouth only on rare occasions.

There's a migration of parents and children to the main aisle, everyone gathering up their sheep costumes and winter boots, discussing whose casserole is up next at the reception, or who will brave the drifting roads to get home first. I catch flashes of conversations: Someone congratulating my mother on "her girl," someone else gossiping about the snowplow effort as if it's the Olympics.

After a few rounds of photos and a heroic rescue of Ben from entrapment in the nativity stable (he declared it "historically accurate" that Wise Men get stuck sometimes), the crowd begins to thin. My mother hovers, orchestrating farewells and ferrying leftover cookies to the kitchen, while my dad stands back, hands in his pockets, surveying the aftermath with satisfaction. I'm still emotional from the show when dad finds me near the back of the sanctuary.

"Walk with me, kiddo?" Dad asks—his voice quiet, but the invitation is huge.

I follow him down the aisle, the hush of the sanctuary wrapping around us now that the crowd is mostly gone and just a few candle flames are left trembling above the altar. Dad doesn't say anything right away. He just walks, slow and even, running a hand along the back of each pew as if counting blessings, or disappointments, or years since he last spent time with his whole family in church.

We stop just in front of the stage. I feel the sweep of every emotion waiting behind my ribs, a tide held back all night by sheer force of will. The nearness of him—his presence, that note of un-shakeable calm—cracks me wide open, and I'm six or sixteen or thirty-two again, it doesn't matter, because I lean right into him and let myself shake.

Dad's arms wrap around me, steady as the northern star. The tears start, slow at first, then all at once—how embarrassing, but also how necessary, here under the blue-shadowed rafters and the echoing ghosts of "Silent Night." I don't try to talk; it's all I can do to keep from falling to the floor and just howling until my lungs explode. For the longest time, Dad doesn't say a word. He just stands there, holding me together, soaking up everything I can't articulate. There are no words for the way these past days have pulled me back through every unfinished wound and let me land, somehow, still breathing. The ache in my chest is enormous—a decades-long backlog of guilt and hope and everything in between.

When I finally manage, "I'm sorry," it comes out in a banshee wheeze.

"Sorry for what, exactly?" I realize Dad's voice is quivering, too.

Is he crying? Dad is not a crier. He likes his feelings the way he likes his coffee: hot, black, and left to cool on its own terms.

I press my face into his shoulder, words spilling out in a slurry: "For everything, I guess. For hurting you. For coming back and making you revisit all this stuff. For not believing—for thinking that if people knew the real me, they'd never..." I can't finish the sentence.

Dad's beard pricks my forehead as he breathes in slowly, ragged, and holds me tighter. "Tess," he says, "Honey...that whole show was you. And I don't mean the part with the paint on your face. I mean the heart that lit up every single person in this room tonight. You never stopped believing, even when you thought you did. I know it. I see it."

He pulls back to look at me, eyes shining in a way that terrifies me with its vulnerability. "You've always been my stubborn, beautiful girl. A little lost now and then, but never unloved. Not by us. And not by...God, either."

"Does it...do you think it counts, though? I mean, when you've done everything wrong, when you don't even know what you believe anymore?" The words are thin and reedy. "Does He still love me? For real, or just, you know, technically?"

Dad's mouth pulls into a line. There's a beat of silence as he wipes at his own cheek for a second before he speaks. "I think you answered that for yourself, up there tonight. Didn't you hear it?"

I open my mouth, then close it, the words stuck in my throat waiting for a push. The moment replays in my mind—me, crouched next to Lily, saying, "Don't be afraid," and meaning for both of us. The line I fed her—"good news of great joy, for *all* people"—echoes now, a simple, blunt-force truth that makes my face hot.

I hear it now, as plain as a pulse—good news, for all people. My throat closes, not with panic this time, but with the strange, sudden possibility that everything

Brayden and my father and even Mabel had coaxed at the edges of my doubt might actually be true. That maybe, just maybe, it never was about stacking up enough good decisions on the cosmic scale to buy my way back into acceptance. That God didn't send Christ as a test—but as a rescue.

He is the love in the heart of all this—in the heart of my ridiculousness, the heart of my family, and in the heart of this imperfect church. Jesus—the heart of God himself—would still cover me. Still find me. Still claim me. No matter what I've done. *I am loved and forgiven.*

It lands with such force that I almost double over, my arms tightening around Dad's waist, anchoring me to the floor so I don't get swept off by the realization that every-thing—every disaster, every shame spiral, every hollow attempt to make myself worthy—was always met with a love that does not waver, even when I do. It's so obvious and so impossible. Dad, arms around me, steady as gran-ite, is not loving me because I succeeded. He is loving me because I am his. And suddenly I see the shape of all those sermons I half-listened to, all the forgiveness I doubted, and how small I made my heart, how small I made God, and how simple the answer had always been. I lean into Dad and let the tears—hot and embarrassing but somehow sweet—claim the space between us. He stands with me until my shuddering goes slack, until the sobs have ebbed into regular breathing once again.

He presses his huge hands on my shoulders, with a gentleness that reminds me of childhood, and brings his face close to mine. "Welcome home, Tess," he whispers. "Welcome home."

Sixteen

It's after midnight when we shake loose of the last hugs, the final low-key oohs and ahhs about the pageant, and the lingering moral support from my parents as they head out for "one more cup of decaf and a Christmas cookie" back at the house. The church settles into stillness, with only the heater's gentle sigh and the rhythmic scrape of a snow shovel outside—some dedicated deacon refusing to surrender to the storm. Lauren Daigle's "Noel" has long since faded from the speakers, but the melody clings to me, echoing a sound of worship that won't quite dissolve.

I spot Brayden waiting for me at the edge of the parking lot, hands jammed in his pockets, chin tucked to his chest. The world is lit up white from the porch lights, every surface sparkling, and somehow Brayden looks both at home and completely untethered.

I walk toward him, boots crunching on the salted sidewalk, and before I can say a word, he lifts his head. His nose is red, his eyes a little tired, but when he sees me, it's like someone's switched on every string of lights in the county. There's something different here—a goodness so palpable it makes my hands shake.

He doesn't move right away. Just stands there, watching as I cross the snowy lot to where he waits. It strikes me how long I've been walking away from good things, how often I've let my heart calcify because it was easier than risking the leap. Brayden's breath comes out ragged and white in the cold, and I realize I want to stand here with him in the raw air forever.

He clears his throat, a little shaky. "S'pose you're officially the town hero now," he says, his voice thick with amusement and something else, almost reverence.

I laugh. "Don't count on it. I'm still on Nancy's blacklist for emergency pageant intervention."

Brayden steps closer, boots crunching on the ice, and I feel the static crackle between us. He hesitates, then says,"I've gotta be honest. I thought you'd be on a flight back to New York before the candles burned out." He's trying for light, but the words wobble with hope. "Didn't figure you'd stick around for the afterparty."

I kick at a snow drift, my cheeks burn, and I trace my boot through the salt. "Let's just say I'm learning to manage my exits with a little more flair these days."

There's a silence, warm and embarrassing, and I look up to find him grinning, not moving. He smiles in this private, amazed way, like he's looking at something rare.

"I don't know how you pull it off, Somerset. Just when I think you're about to make a run for it, you..." He tilts his head, like he's reading the last line of a story only he can see. "You stick the landing."

I shiver, though I'm not cold. "World's full of surprises," I say, but my voice is thinner than I'd like, because nothing in my life—nothing—has prepared me for the way Brayden is looking at me now.

He closes the space between us in two long strides, snow spraying from the treads of his boots. I brace for the old joke or the well-timed one-liner, but he just looks at me, long and straightforward. "You okay?" he asks. Not the casual, automatic "you okay?" people toss off, but the careful kind, the kind that means, "You can tell me the truth and I won't run from it."

I know what he's really asking. Not about the cold, not about tonight, but about the thing that's rattled inside me since I set foot in Maple Ridge. There's a time when I would have deflected with a joke, or made a show of being invulnerable, but that armor feels hilariously pointless now.

So I tell him the truth. "I think I finally get it," I say, and it sounds simple, but just saying it makes my throat close up again. "Ever since that night, I thought forgiveness was, something you just sort of... earned? Like, eventually you log enough decades of regret and—poof—God checks off the box and you're allowed to stop hating yourself. But that's not it at all."

Brayden's smile falters, but he stays close, his eyes fixed on mine. This is it, the moment to get the words right, and for once I don't want to blow it.

"When I was in the sanctuary with my dad—just, you know, breaking down emotionally—it finally made sense. My whole life, I've been measuring myself against this standard, right? Like if you're good enough, or sorry enough, you get to be loved again." I take a deep breath before continuing. "But He...God... doesn't play by the same rules. He just...loves you. Because you're His. He wants you as you are."

Brayden's smile returns, like he knew I would come to this conclusion all along. He just nods his head, waiting for me to continue.

"I'm not saying I've got it figured out. But I'm done try-ing to martyr myself. Maybe I don't have to keep proving I'm sorry, or sacrifice every good thing in my life as some kind of penance. Maybe I just...accept His love, and see what happens." I say it quiet, but I mean it. So much so, it actually hurts to breathe.

Brayden doesn't answer with a sermon or a Bible verse or any of the things a normal person might expect from a pastor. He just steps forward, closes the final handful of inches, and pulls me into his arms. The move is so sudden—so completely not Brayden, or maybe entirely, deeply Brayden—that it takes my brain a few seconds to catch up. My cheek presses against the rough wool of his coat, and for the first time in I don't know how many years, I feel what it's like to be just...held. Not fixed, not improved, not condescended to or pitied. Just held.

I allow myself to let go—the tension of years, the part of me always poised for pain or deflection or disaster. It all unspools in the circle of his arms.

And I almost lose it, right there in the salted parking lot. *Nope... I'm not going to cry.*

I feel relief so overwhelming it feels like the sharp edge of hope. my head rests on Brayden's chest, his hands strong and careful in their hold. I wonder how long I could stay here, boxed in by the cold and the silence and his arms. *Eternity would not be long enough.*

Brayden pulls back first, just enough to take my face in with that searching look he's always had. Like he's cataloging every detail for later, as if the whole world might vanish before sunrise. Then he breathes a small laugh, glances up at the wild, dark blue sky overhead, and without another word, slides his gloveless hand into mine.

His palm is rough with cold and callus, but the touch itself is gentle. We start walking, the two of us side by side, boots leaving twin tracks toward Main Street.

The world is ridiculously, impossibly perfect, blanketed in fresh snow that's still untouched except for the two-track path we're making, one bootprint at a time. The sky is that clear, brittle sapphire you only get in a Montana winter, the stars bolder and closer than any city sky could ever allow. We walk for a while without talking, our hands knitted together and swinging a little, like this is an ordinary night and not the first evening of the rest of my life.

Brayden takes the lead as he heads towards Main and cuts across the church's adjacent field—a shortcut to nowhere.

He lengthens his stride, hand tightening on mine. Past the last puddle of porch light, the stars are the only light and everything besides our breath feels imaginary. The only real things are the cold, and the sound of us moving together, and the glow of memory—brighter, somehow, with every step.

It takes me a second to realize Brayden's headed for the old tree line at the edge of the church property, that pocket of cottonwoods and chokecherry bramble where we used to escape Sunday School and share contraband snacks. The treehouse—is still there in the old tree battered by thirteen winters—an old fortress of plywood and stubborn dreams halfway up the trunk of our favorite oak. Only now, there's a strand of lights curling up the ladder, colorful and hopeful in led splendor.

Something catches in my chest. That first night back in town I stood at the edge of the church property, staring at it—a dark silhouette against the illuminated church windows of Grace Hollow. It was like seeing a ghost of us, preserved in wood and memory, before I'd even laid eyes on the man Brayden had become. And just like that night, all the old memories of us together rush back—Brayden holding me and all the promise of a future together.

The closer we get, the brighter the string of lights. There's a makeshift handrail lashed on with cable ties, a fresh plank over the ladder's missing rung I remember snapping off our senior summer, and at the top platform—two ancient camping chairs, waiting. I stop at the foot of the tree. Brayden doesn't hesitate. He puts his foot on the ladder, dead-set on climbing, boot-to-plank, hand-over-hand, like he's done it a hundred times since I left.

A laugh catches in my throat. "Is this structurally sound?"

He looks over his shoulder, winks. "I did a load test. Meets all modern safety codes," he says, and then he's up, two steps at a time, his silhouette a shadow lit only by the bright sky.

If there was any question left in my mind as to whether this was real—the night, the reconciliation, the Brayden who never completely left my life—it dissolves with every rung I climb. The treehouse is smaller than I remember it, the hatch tighter, but the moment I pop through the floor, I'm drowned in an unruly flood of nostalgia. The old "Keep Out!" sign is still nailed awkwardly to the wall, only a little older, a little weathered, but this time, right underneath it, someone (Brayden, obviously) had scribbled in Sharpie: "Except Tess."

Brayden had cleared out the debris, patched the roof—he even stashed an emergency blanket and two mugs in a wooden box. The Christmas lights ring the inside beams, and in the warmth of their light, the whole world outside feels distant and impossible.

I'm so startled it comes out as a laugh, and Brayden, already perched in one of the chairs, just shrugs and says, "Truth is, I never changed that sign after you left."

I run my gloved finger over the fading Sharpie. "This is..." I start, but the words jam, because how do you explain what it's like to step back into your prequel, only to find someone's been dusting the set, all these years and then some?

He pats the chair beside him, and when I sit, the ancient wood creaks but doesn't give. We're close, knee-to-knee, and the familiar feel of tree bark against my back feels weirdly safe, like nothing terrible could happen here—not in this patch of time, not under the bright Christmas lights and a sky that looks close enough to touch.

He's quiet, but it's not the uneasy kind—it's expectation, a silence built to hold something precious, waiting out the clamor of the world until only the real stuff is left. "Not bad, huh?" he says at last, deadpan, like he's inviting me to critique a painting. I smile, running my glove over the battered plywood floor. "Not bad?" I echo. "Brayden, this is a Christmas architectural achievement. I'm pretty sure I still have the original splinters in my thigh from fourth grade. You even fixed the ladder. How is this still here?"

He props his boots on the crossbeam, arms slung loose around his knees, staring out at the field. "Maybe because I could never quite bring myself to let it go," he says, voice light but edged with something sharp and honest. "Sometimes, I come out here after a rough board meeting or a funeral...or just when I want to disappear." He glances sideways, sheepish. "Sometimes I hope some kid will stumble on it, and they'll think it's magic, like we did. But mostly I just...keep it from falling down."

He's not looking at me as he says it, but I can read every word in the tight set of his jaw, the way his boot taps a slow rhythm on the treehouse floor. How many nights did he climb up here, sitting in the weathered chair and tracing his own footprints over the years, armoring up for another round with the world? "Sometimes I bring my Bible and a flashlight, sometimes it's just me and my thoughts." He looks up at the rafters, voice impossibly small for how big it feels inside me. "I guess it's always been easier to talk to God up here." I want to ask why, but the answer's already written in the way the cold goes softer, the way the distant light from Maple Ridge glimmers up through the branches. This was our sanctuary away from the bigger one across the field. Brayden picks at a fraying end of the wool blanket, unspooling the loose thread.

I want to reach out, to wrap my arms around his neck and ask if this is his way of remembering, of holding on, of not letting me go even when it was obvious I was gone. But I don't. Instead I just look at him, the way the shifting green and red light gives his face a strange sort of youth—almost the same as the kid from a million late-night dare sessions and whispered secrets. He glances at me, eyebrow up. "I know it's silly, keeping this thing alive," he says, "but I didn't want to let it go. Not until you saw what we'd built, one more time." He means the treehouse, but I know it's so much more.

His hands fidget with the blanket again, the silence between us delicate and unscripted. Then he glances up—not just a peek, but a real, searching look that lands so hard I flinch a little. "I'm glad you came back," he says, as if the words have spent years trapped behind his teeth and tonight's the only chance they'll get out. "I mean—not just for the pageant, or your folks. I mean you. I always hoped you'd find your way back," he says, voice catching near the end. "All of you."

There's a small pause, the kind that might last forever if nobody risks the next breath. The air is thin up here, and the lights from the church feel decades away. Brayden's hand hovers on the edge of the blanket, and I realize that he's not just been keeping this treehouse alive for nostalgia's sake.

He's been coming out here for hope. *For me.*

All those years, while I was speed-running my way through New York and med school and every self-imposed punishment I could invent, Brayden was up here, patching boards and taping up leaks, making this place ready for the day when God would answer his prayers.

He looks away, like it costs him a physical effort, but then he's looking back, the way he does—direct, blue as morning, zero filters. "I know I talked a lot about my *own* journey of healing and forgiveness, but...I didn't pray for you to come home just so it would make things okay for us, or to fix my own stuff. I prayed..." He lets out a choked laugh and looks up at the roof, blinking. "I prayed you'd find your way, Tess—like I did. That you'd know how loved you are, by Him even more than me. That you'd get what it means to be wanted and whole and free." He laughs again, but it's shaky—an exhale that fogs and dissolves in the cold. "You don't have to say anything. I just wanted you to know." It's so tender it nearly undoes every defense I have left.

"You prayed for me," I say, because I have to hear it out loud. Brayden shrugs, but he can't keep the tremor out of his voice. "Every day. I mean, sometimes just the simple ones...

'God, please get her home safe, or show her she's not alone.' Sometimes...more. Sometimes the only way I knew I loved you was because I couldn't not pray for you. Not just for you to come back here—not just to me. But to Him. To yourself." His voice breaks, and it's not embarrassment—he lets it. The silence afterward is full of everything I never dared say.

I sit so still I'm afraid I'll break the world if I move, my eyes hitching from the battered handrail to the stars through the window, to the man who, in spite of every-thing, never stopped waiting for me to come home.

I want to say it—the thing that's been burning a hole in my chest since the moment I saw him on the first night, since every argument and every note of forgiveness that's played between us in this small town and under these winter skies. But for once, I don't have to. The look on my face must say it all. Brayden's hand, warm, finds mine on the edge of the blanket and holds it, simple and sure.

So I say the only thing that's left. "I missed you," I whisper. "More than I ever let myself know."

Seventeen

C hristmas morning comes on quietly, like someone tucking in a blanket. Morning light filters through my childhood bedroom window, casting honey-colored squares across my pillow through the decades-old glass. For the first time in forever, I wake up in my own house, in my own bed, and I'm not immediately dreading what waits beyond the door. Instead, there's this slow, warmth seeping through me—a kind of peace I forgot existed.

The ceiling still has the constellation stickers from when I was thirteen and obsessed with space, a few of them half-peeled but stubbornly luminous. The old bookshelf are still filled with my old school books and battered novels, and next to it is the dresser I once Sharpied with every dumb inside joke from high school. The carpet's worn flat in the patch by the window where

I used to camp out with a notebook, planning my big escape. Somehow, the room is smaller, or maybe I'm just finally big enough to fit in it.

From downstairs comes the faint clatter of pans and the muted hum of my mother's Christmas music—Micheal W. Smith and Carrie Underwood singing "All is Well," barely louder than the soft hiss of radiators. The smells come next: cinnamon rolls with extra icing, coffee with that burnt edge, and a note of bacon so sharp I can almost hear it.

For a while I just lie there, letting the stillness wrap around me, cataloging the feeling of belonging as if it's a new symptom I'm studying for the first time.

Eventually, the draw of caffeine and curiosity gets me up. I shuffle to the closet and dig out the fleece robe Mom insists is "practically vintage" because she bought it at the original Target in Billings. The slippers are hospital-issue, brought home with me like a favorite teddy bear, now threadbare but loyal.

When I pad down the hallway, I pause at the landing. The Christmas tree is visible from here—lights twinkling through the banister, the bottom third crowded with a last-minute cluster of wrapped presents. It's all there—the ornaments made of pasta, the handprint reindeer, the one glass angel that always loses its wings by December 25th. There's even a smattering of tinsel that Mom pretends to hate but always hangs anyway.

The kitchen is a living, breathing thing this morning. Mom— already in her signature red apron—moves between stove and counter like she's running a triage unit, but with more humming and fewer panicked interns. Her hair is pinned back in a way that means business. She spots me immediately, her eyes softening in that split second before she goes full maternal.

"Good morning, sleepyhead," she says, voice bright enough to compete with the tree. "Merry Christmas! I hope you slept well. You want orange juice, or is it coffee?"

"Coffee," I croak, and she grins, already pouring.

Dad is at the kitchen table, a fortress of newspaper sections fanned out around him. He's in a flannel shirt and those jeans he claims are his "off-duty uniform," glasses perched low on his nose. There's a crossword half-completed, and next to it, a small pile of opened mail—one of them looking suspiciously like EKG readings—sorted in Dad's meticulous fashion.

He barely glances up as I settle into the chair across from him, but I catch the twitch of a smile before he shields it behind the sports section. "Morning," he says. "Coffee's hot. Don't let your mother overdose you on cinnamon rolls...you'll be in a diabetic coma after one of those."

I accept the mug from Mom, who ruffles my hair like I'm seven and then sits beside me, close enough that our arms brush. The kitchen is too warm, but it's...cozy. Like the world has stopped spinning just for this.

For a few minutes, there's only the sound of chewing, pages flipping, and Mom's gentle running commentary on the weather, "Can you believe they're saying another storm next week?" and the state of the casserole dishes she's borrowed from the neighbors "That Mabel, I swear, she can bake for an army."

Dad reads in good-natured silence, then passes me the comics as if it's still our tradition.

When Mom finally brings the food—eggs, bacon, cinnamon rolls hot enough to blister your tongue—it's more than enough for three people. She fusses, as always, over portion sizes and salt content, and Dad mutters about the cholesterol only after Mom's out of earshot. It's so wonderfully, impossibly normal.

We eat for a while, the conversation meandering from town gossip to the finer points of pie crust. I'm halfway through a third roll, dangerously close to a diabetic event, when Dad puts down his fork and clears his throat.

It's the kind of throat-clearing that means business, and even Mom stops mid-sentence, hands folded in her lap.

"I got the results yesterday," he says. He doesn't look at me, or at Mom, just at the empty space above the coffee carafe. "The CT scan, and the blood work. Doctor Rosenblatt called just before the pageant." His fingers drum once on the table before curling into a fist.

A silence wedges itself between the Christmas plates, sudden and absolute.

Mom's face is unreadable, but she doesn't speak. I grip my mug, bracing.

Dad's voice is steady, but there's something in it—maybe relief, maybe just exhaustion. "My heart is fine. The EKG is normal. They want me to follow-up, but the numbers from the stress-test are good. I'm fine." He lets out a shaky breath, like he's been holding it for months.

I stare at him, waiting for the punchline, the second shoe, the qualifier. There isn't one.

Mom bursts into laughter—the kind that says she's been holding a secret—then folds me into her arms until I can feel her heart hammering against mine.

Dad watches us from behind his coffee mug, his mouth a straight line but his eyes crinkling at the corners in that way that, for Frank Somerset, counts as dancing in the streets. "Don't make a scene," he mutters.

I don't realize I'm crying until I blink and a tear lands in my coffee.

Mom straightens, brushing her hands on her apron. "He's going to take it easy from now on," she says, as if the last few minutes never happened. "Less work, more walks with me.

We're even considering switching to the cholesterol-free bacon. Miracles do happen."

A sound escapes me—half sob, half chuckle—catching in my throat before spilling out genuine and unguarded.

Dad goes back to his eggs, but his posture is loose, the line of his shoulders less rigid than I've seen in years. "We'll discuss the bacon." he says, doing his best to keep his mouth from forming a smile.

Breakfast resumes. The air is lighter, the kitchen less crowded by invisible threats. I catch Mom watching Dad over her coffee, and for a second I see what it must have been like when they first met—a pair of nerds, thrown together by fate or college scheduling, falling into step and never looking back. *Thank you God for my family.*

I reach across the table and squeeze Dad's hand. He returns the gesture. For once, we just sit there, three Somersets at a cozy kitchen table, letting the silence be soft instead of awkward. *I just want to stay like this forever.*

After breakfast, with my veins running pure cinnamon roll and the mood still giddy from the news, I escape upstairs for a breather. But instead of flopping back into bed, I find myself wandering down the carpet runner to the corner room—Dad's home office. The door is slightly ajar, the handle worn shiny by decades of habitual twisting.

I push it open and step into a museum of order and low-key bravado. The desk, a tank of oak and brass, sits dead center, everything on its surface lined up with surgical precision: pens in a tray, prescription pad perfectly squared, a mug with "World's Best Dad" (my gift, age twelve) right where it's always been. On the left, a shelf hosts binders labeled in Dad's handwriting, each labeled with the years—like "2002: THE GREAT COUGHING PLAGUE" and "2020: COVID." There's even a bottle of sanitizer. A little reminder of the worst time in our medical profession's history.

But what pulls me in is the wall opposite the desk.

It's covered, chair-rail to ceiling, in framed stuff. I mean, all of it—certificates, diplomas, a smattering of blue and gold ribbons from science fairs that happened before I even hit puberty. There's my high school graduation picture (awkward bangs, forced smile), a clipping from the Maple Ridge Gazette about my "Young Humanitarian" award for organizing a sock drive, even the campus map from my first semester at Columbia, annotated in Dad's impossible chicken-scratch. Centered at eye level is Columbia's commencement program from when I graduated med school—only a parent would bother to find, and then have it matted.

There's no logic to the arrangement except this: it is all me, every misfit year and nerd achievement and small-town win, immortalized and hung with equal importance. No hierarchy. Just Tess, everywhere.

I trail my fingers along the glass of a certificate—Maple Ridge Community Service, 1999. The next frame holds a grainy photo of me, age fifteen, clutching a blue ribbon with both fists and wearing the world's ugliest cargo pants. Dad had written "Reluctant winner" under it in Sharpie, like a label for a rare animal.

I swallow hard.

Behind me, I catch the sound of a footstep. I turn, and Dad stands in the doorway. He doesn't say anything, just folds his arms and watches me, expression unreadable.

I gesture at the wall. "Why...did you keep all this?"

He glances at the display, like he's seeing it for the first time, then shrugs—classic Dad. "You're my daughter," he says, as if that explains everything. And to him, it does.

I can't speak. I look at the wall again, at the way the certificates are perfectly aligned, each one dusted and cared for, as if they are his prized possessions.

He steps into the office, hands in pockets. "Your mother said it was obsessive," he admits, eyes fixed on a diploma I'd nearly flunked out of sophomore year to earn. "But

I figured...someday you'd need to be reminded of how special you are to me. You were always my hero."

I nod, not trusting my voice. The lump in my throat is the size of a snowball.

He watches me for a long moment, then clears his throat. "Like I said back at the church...I'm proud of you, Tess." The words come out rough, like he was getting choked up. "Always have been. Even when you were a brat."

I snort, and it helps.

He steps closer, not quite a hug but almost. "I always knew you'd be a success," he says. "But I also knew you'd find your way back. Even though you didn't know it yourself."

I stand there, letting the moment settle, cataloging the pride and the love and all the things we never put into words. Then, finally, I meet his eyes and say, "Thanks, Dad." It's a simple thing, but it holds more than every trophy on the wall.

He nods, businesslike. "You're welcome."

Then, after a quick side-hug, he turns and leaves me alone with my own history, the door swinging shut with a soft click.

I look at the wall again. For the first time, it feels less like a ledger of what I owe and more like a promise—one I'm finally ready to keep.

I'm still staring at the wall of my past achieve-ments—cringing at the science fair photo where my braces caught the flash, smiling at the spelling bee cer-tificate with my name in gold lettering— when the door-bell's chime cuts through my nostalgia. The sound is a crisp jolt against the hush of the morning. My heart skips, then races ahead of my thoughts—but for once, the flut-ter in my chest feels like Christmas morning excitement, not the usual fight-or-flight.

I cross the house in two seconds flat. The door glass is fogged at the edges, but I don't even need to squint to see Brayden on the other side, standing on the stoop, arms loaded with presents. He's wearing a flannel shirt and the boots he claims are appropriate for every season, which is the kind of practical logic that makes me want to both punch and kiss him.

He flashes an apologetic, sheepish grin as I open the door. "Merry Christmas," he says, his voice breathless from the cold, or maybe the load of gifts, or maybe some-thing else entirely.

"Wow," I say, "is this a toy drive, or are you auditioning for Santa?"

He shrugs, shifting the packages into one arm. "It's all regifting, so don't get excited." But his eyes tell me he is being funny.

I wave him in, and Mom appears from the kitchen, a look of delight on her face that's only ever reserved for church babies and high school graduations. "Oh, Bray-den! You made it," she sings, and before he can set any-thing down, she's drawing him into a hug that looks like she hasn't seen him in years.

Dad hangs back at the corner, but even he can't maintain his regular poker face. He offers a hand, which Brayden takes with the kind of grip reserved for job interviews and parentals who still intimidate you. "Welcome," Dad says, low and level, but there's a smile ghosting the edges.

Brayden sheds his coat and follows me to the living room, the gifts rattling in his arms. Mom hustles to the kitchen for more coffee, and Dad disappears, presumably to make sure the TV is set to the correct "parade channel" (or maybe just another round of A Christmas Story). For a minute, it's just me and Brayden, and the air between us crackles with a kind of new excitement.

He sets the packages under the tree with exaggerated care. "I hope I didn't overdo it," he mutters, scanning the rest of the presents.

I look at him, really look, and for the first time in years, I'm leaning into whatever comes next. "You didn't," I say, and it's true. The morning already feels like a fever dream, but this— him, here, with me—is exactly what I want.

Mom calls from the kitchen, "Come in and get warm, both of you!" so we do. She hands Brayden a mug the size of a soup bowl and piles him with cinnamon rolls before he can protest. He takes it all in stride, and I'm not sure if he's always been this good at fitting in, or if I just never noticed.

When Dad returns, he's got the air of a man preparing for the Olympics—he's set the living room with two remotes, three fleece blankets, and a tray of mixed nuts. He gestures at the tree, a not-so-subtle nudge for presents to be opened sooner rather than later.

The gift exchange is a study in family choreography. We take turns, like always: youngest to oldest, then reverse, then wild- card as soon as Mom decides the formalities are too slow. The wrapping paper multiplies into drifts on the carpet, and the bows ricochet off every surface, each one punctuated by Mom's, "Save that for next year!" and Dad's, "She says that every time, but we never do."

Brayden's gifts are...hilarious, in the best way. For Dad, a deluxe set of hand-tied fishing lures—probably chosen by the hardware store clerk, but Dad handles each one like it's a holy relic. For Mom, a cookbook from some micro-famous Montana chef, signed with a note that's so heartfelt Mom tears up reading it. "How did you—" she starts, and Brayden shrugs, looking bashful. "You've been feeding the church for years," he says. "It seemed fair to return the favor."

He hands me a flat, awkwardly wrapped box last. The paper is uneven at the edges, the tape job surgical but excessive. I peel it open, and inside is a journal, heavy and leather-bound, its cover stamped with my initials. A tag is tucked in the front: "For the next chapter. Write a beautiful story." Underneath, a second package—a slim, travel-size Bible. The pages are onion-skin thin, but the cover is soft and worn. "I used it a lot in college," he says, eyes low. "I wanted you to have it."

My breath catches. For a second, time stands still—like this single, ordinary moment is actually the pivot point for the rest of my life.

Mom beams at the two of us like she orchestrated this entire tableau, and Dad leans back in his chair, eyeing the gifts with a look of silent approval. The light from the Christmas tree flickers across the room, painting everyone in gold and green, the glow brighter than any bulb on Main Street.

There's a peace in the room that I never knew how to name, not really. But now, surrounded by torn wrapping paper and the familiar pulse of my family, I get it. This—messy, noisy, perfectly imperfect—is what I was always running from and what I've been running toward. The gift isn't the things on the floor—it's what God gave me: the people, the laughter, and the fact that, for the first time ever, I belong exactly where I am.

At some point, Mom whisks off to the kitchen. "I have to start the ham, or we'll be eating at midnight!"

Dad vanishes to "test" the recliner in the den, which is code for catching a nap before anyone can assign him chores. Brayden and I are left alone, the wrapping paper sea rising around our ankles.

He looks at me, half-smile in place, and nudges the Bible toward my lap. "My notes from college are in it," he says. "So if you need help understanding a passage...I'll be right there with you."

I don't trust my voice, so I just nod, pressing my palm over the cover. The weight of it is real, comforting.

After a minute, Brayden says, "The words in this Bible are your anchor. Everything you need is in this book. It will remind you who Jesus is and how deeply He loves you."

I look at him, and the words come easier than I expect. "I meant what I said last night...I've missed you all along," I pause, thinking carefully of what to say next.

"Thank you...not just for the Bible, but for...not giving up on me...this is where I'm supposed to be. All this time, I thought I'd lost God...and you. And now, it feels like He's giving me both back."

He grins, and swallows hard, "I wanted to give you something you can hold onto when doubts try to creep back in." His voice softens, a hint of emotion breaking through. "As for me...I can't tell you how good it is just to see you here, with Him again. I never stopped hoping you'd find your way back. And maybe..." his eyes meet mine, steady but searching, "maybe even back here...to me."

There's a lull in the noise—a stillness that's not awkward, but companionable. I lean over, careful not to knock the coffee onto the couch, and rest my head against Brayden's shoulder.

"Thank you," I whisper, just for him and God. "For second chances. For answered prayers."

He squeezes my hand, gentle but certain.

For the first time since I left Maple Ridge, I feel it—an ache gone quiet, a heart put back together, a place at the table with my name on it. There's no dramatic music, no spotlight, just this: a second chance, a morning full of light, and the knowledge that I am—finally and completely—home.

Eighteen

Two days after Christmas, Maple Ridge wakes from its snow- bound coma and throws a festival like the world never ended. Main Street is plowed clean and then some, the banks of snow so high on either side it's like walking through the set of a winter musical—maybe the exact one the town kids will perform, if they ever get the community center unlocked again. Every old-fashioned lamp post is wound with a spiral of white lights and draped with garlands, and it's hard to tell where the frost ends and the LED glow begins.

Brayden and I park the Jeep two blocks down, then make our way, hand in hand, toward the epicenter. The air bites at every patch of exposed skin, but there's a new warmth under it—a kind of pulse that picks up with every step. I catch us in a store window and it's a little embarrassing: two grown adults holding hands like we're at prom. But the best part? Neither of us lets go.

The festival is exactly what you'd expect from a town that lives for Christmas and has spent the better part of the week snowed in. The vendor stalls are back-to-back, wedged along the cleared sidewalk, each one advertising something both incredibly homemade and borderline hazardous to your cholesterol: fudge, caramel corn, candied nuts, marshmallow monstrosities. There's a line for roasted almonds (which I'm convinced are the best treat on the planet), and another for kettle corn that smells so sweet it's like an assault.

Kids in fleece hats dart between booths, shrieking in that hypothermia-resistant way only Montana children can. At the end of the block, a carousel cobbled together from what looks like repurposed farm equipment creaks and whirls, its chipped paint horses rising and falling with mechanical determination. The bandstand—nothing more than a flatbed truck dressed in drooping tinsel—blares The Eagles' "Please Come Home for Christmas" through speakers that have seen better decades. I catch myself laughing at the irony of the old song. The "Santa" is Mabel's nephew in a glued-on beard, passing out candy canes and joking with anyone who'll listen.

It would all be perfect, if I didn't have the creeping suspicion that every single person here is waiting to see whether I'll start a fire, get into a fistfight, or just run for the state line.

The first thing I notice as we hit the heart of Main is the side- eyes. They slide to us, then away, then snap right back when they think we're not looking. I recognize almost every face in the crowd, which means every face recognizes me. I see the double takes, the nudges, the whispered commentary—some subtle, most not. One older woman in a faux-fur hat does an honest-to-God sign of the cross when I pass. She's holding a chihuahua in a matching sweater, so I don't take it personally.

The funny thing is, I expected the stares, the prelude to drama. What I didn't expect is how much of the staring is just curiosity, not malice. There's a difference in the set of people's jaws: not judgment, just... watching. As if they're waiting to see what I'll do next, but not hoping for disaster.

Brayden must sense my tension, because his thumb starts a slow, soothing circle on the back of my hand. He's in full small- town pastor mode tonight: boots, pressed flannel under his wool coat, hair tamed within an inch of its life. The only giveaway is the scrape on his cheek (he says it's from the church window incident, but I suspect a mishap with a ladder and a string of Christmas lights).

He leans down, voice pitched just for me. "You doing okay?" I squeeze his hand, but my words come out thin. "I feel like I'm about to be called up for a talent show I never auditioned for."

He laughs. "Relax, you're the guest of honor. Maple Ridge loves a good redemption arc."

I roll my eyes but the phrase sticks—redemption arc. It sounds nice, if a little dramatic. We push on.

We're about halfway to the bandstand when the first direct approach happens. It's a young mom—maybe my age, and she's got a toddler on her hip and a mittened kid tugging at her jacket. When she catches up, she gives Brayden a quick hello, but the real target is me.

"Tess, right? I'm so glad you're back," she says, her smile shy but real. "My sister remembers you from...well, from way back. Welcome home." The words are simple, but the relief in her face is unmistakable—like she's been wanting to say them for a while and only just got permission. Before I can reply, she's swept off by her kids, but I stand there for a second, floored.

Brayden grins. "Told you," he says, as if he orchestrated the encounter.

We move through the vendor stalls, and with each step, the weight in my chest shifts. At first it was the burn of scrutiny, but now it's a little lighter—like curiosity with a side of goodwill. I recognize people from Grace Hollow, the grocery store, the one Mexican restaurant in town. There's a pattern to the interactions: first, the glance; next, the quick flash of recognition; finally, a smile—sometimes awkward, sometimes so earnest it makes my eyes sting.

An old teacher of mine (retired now, but still notorious for her evil pop quizzes) waves us over. "You look wonderful, dear," she says. "We always knew you'd do something amazing." I'm pretty sure she's confusing me with someone else, but I don't correct her. The point is, she's saying it at all.

We're about three booths in when Brayden tugs me toward a tent with a hand-lettered sign: "JESUS, JOY, & JAVA." Inside, it's the church ladies, presiding over row after row of steaming pots of coffee and hot chocolate. The tent is buzzing with laughter—not the cutthroat energy of a city coffee bar but the warm, gossipy hum of people who have decided to like each other for the night.

As we step in, a hush falls—not judgmental, just surprised. The woman at the head of the line is Nancy, in a scarf that could double as a flotation device. She fixes me with a look that is half warning, half curiosity, but then she says, "We're doing the marshmallow option tonight—one or two?" I blink. "Two, please?"

She drops them in, then, in a move so unexpected it short- circuits my brain, adds a third. "I won't tell if you don't," she says, handing over the cup.

I take it, hands trembling just a little. The heat seeps through the cup and into my fingers, and suddenly I have to work to keep my face composed. I thank her, voice quivering, and Brayden wraps an arm around my shoulder.

As we step out into the icy air, I blink hard. Brayden tilts his head, searching my face. "Hey," he says, voice low, "You did it. You made it through the gauntlet." There's a playful pride in his tone, but also the steady warmth I remember from childhood, the one that could thaw out the worst winter.

"Don't jinx it," I say, but the joke is weak, because all I can think is how much it means—this cup of hot chocolate, this moment, this second chance.

We stand on the edge of Main, backs to the lights, hot chocolate in hand, and for the first time in a long, long time, I feel like I belong. I just want to be here, with him, and let the world keep turning. The festival crowds swirl around us, the music kicks up, and under the white glow of the streetlights, I let myself believe that everything—absolutely everything—might actually turn out okay.

Before I can finish my hot chocolate—or process the whiplash of not being a social leper for the first time since puberty— a familiar cackle cuts through the crowd. Mabel Thompson, church matriarch and reigning champion of the Maple Ridge pie contest, is making a beeline for us, moving at a speed that should not be physically possible given the width of her parka and the length of her cane.

She sweeps right past Brayden and snags me in a hug so sudden my cup nearly flies from my hands. Her arms are surprisingly strong, wrapped around my ribs with a force that's at once maternal and competitive, like she's trying to absorb all my regrets and replace them with the scent of White Shoulders perfume and peppermint.

"Oh, Tess," she says into my ear, her voice trembling just enough to betray the effort. "I always knew you'd come home." There's a click as she leans back and, with the sleight of hand only a true church lady possesses, slips a peppermint from her sleeve and into my palm. She closes my fingers around it, gives a wink. "You did good, dear. You did real good."

My throat clamps shut. I want to say something witty, or at least thank her, but it's like every smart-aleck comeback I've ever prepped just disappears. Instead, I just nod and blink really fast, hoping Mabel will take it as a sign of sincere emotion and not incipient hypothermia.

She pivots to Brayden, jabbing his chest with her cane. "You keep an eye on this one," she says, grinning. "She's trouble. We like trouble around here. Keeps the prayer chain honest." There's a round of laughter from the people within earshot, and I realize Mabel is giving me a gift more precious than any candy—she's putting the gossipers on notice: this one is family, so knock it off.

Mabel turns, scans the crowd, and then—mission accomplished— moves on to the next conversation like a benevolent hurricane.

Brayden grins, face flushed and happy in a way I haven't seen since our treehouse confessional. "I love that woman," he says, shaking his head.

I smirk. "She is a force of nature."

"She is *that*," he replies, and we both laugh, letting the sound ripple out over the carolers and the ring of bells from the next block.

I see Hannah and she's got the kind of smile that lights up a whole zip code. When she finally reaches me, she throws her arms around my neck like there's no tomorrow. "Tess!" she squeals, squeezing so hard my vertebrae realign. The momentum of her hug nearly sloshes what's left of my hot chocolate onto her coat, but she doesn't care. For a second, I'm awkwardly 16 again, but then I realize she's just happy—so happy that for the briefest moment, I forget all the years we fell out of each other's lives.

Before Hannah can say anything her son spots Santa at the end of the block and yanks her coat with such force she nearly falls over.

"SANTA!" he yells, then tugs again.

Hannah, cheeks pink and wind-chapped, turns back and gives me a look that could light up the block. "Text me?" she mouths across the space, then gives a little tap to her phone, like she's swearing me in on a Bible.

I nod, unexpectedly choked up at how easy it is, how much I want to take her up on it. She gets swept away toward Santa, her son a blur in red boots, and I'm left wondering when exactly I started craving these unremarkable, incredible moments of normal.

The moment is so normal, so free of crisis, I almost miss the approach of Sheriff Carl Johnson. He's not in uniform tonight— just a heavy-duty parka and boots big enough to kick down a barn door. But the walk, the jaw, the don't-mess-with-me aura is all there. He's trailed by two deputies, both of whom immediately pretend to be interested in the popcorn booth across the street, because no one in their right mind wants to get caught in a personal conversation with Carl.

He stops directly in front of us, feet braced wide, hands deep in his pockets. He scans Brayden, then me, then back again.

"Evening, Pastor," he says, and though his face is all steel, there's a twinkle in his eyes that would get him cited for unprofessional behavior if anyone were keeping score.

"Evening, Sheriff," Brayden says, matching his tone.

Carl's gaze flicks to me. "Dr. Somerset," he says. "Glad to see you survived the blizzard. And the pageant." His voice is perfectly flat, but I swear there's a smirk hiding in the corners.

I nod, trying not to let my nerves show. "Wouldn't miss it for the world."

He grunts—a single, syllabic communication that can mean anything from 'thank you for your service' to 'stop jaywalking.' He looks around, making a show of surveilling the crowd, then leans in conspiratorially. "You two behave yourselves," he says, eyebrow raised, "or I'll have to put you in the dunk tank at the Fourth of July again."

Brayden laughs, and it's a good one—real, not practiced. "No promises, sir."

Carl steps even closer, and for a second I brace for a lecture or a warning, but instead he claps Brayden on the shoulder, holds him there a beat, and says, low, "You're doing right by them. All of them." He nods at the crowd, then at me. "Don't forget it."

Brayden's smile goes soft, and he nods, just once. "Yes, sir," he says.

The exchange is over in a heartbeat, but the meaning radiates out like a weather front. Carl isn't just giving Brayden a personal blessing—he's making it known to everyone within earshot that the new order is sanctioned, official, and not up for debate.

As if on cue, the next wave of neighbors approaches: a retired mailman with a talent for dad jokes, an older couple who once chaperoned every youth lock-in at Grace Hollow, the middle- school science teacher who once caught me swiping Bunsen burners for a home experiment. They all stop, shake hands, say welcome back, and it's like the rules of social quarantine have lifted, the thaw spreading one smile at a time.

There's a moment, as I stand in the center of this little knot of warmth and human noise, that I realize how much I've wanted this—not the approval, exactly, but the feeling of being a part of something that doesn't need to be earned every day. For years, I thought being strong meant keeping everyone at a safe distance, because then it hurt less when the world turned. But here, in the shadow of the blinking bandstand and the cloud of powdered sugar rising from the funnel cake tent, I start to believe that maybe belonging is as much about letting yourself be seen as it is about surviving.

I look at Brayden, and he looks at me, and there's this silent conversation—one we've had since forever—where we both agree that this, right here, is the miracle we never saw coming.

We're not outcasts. We're home. *Thank you, Lord.*

The bandstand is the epicenter of the festival and, for tonight at least, the axis of the universe. It's just a raised platform draped in tinsel, but when Brayden takes my hand and pulls me toward it, the crowd splits like he's Moses and the Red Sea is made of puffer jackets and sugar-high kids. At first I think we're just headed for a better vantage point, but as soon as I spot the microphone and the waiting cluster of local officials (including Nancy in full-tilt lipstick), I know, this is more than an excuse to admire the view.

He glances at me as we climb the steps, and I see the flicker of nerves even on him. "You coming?" he murmurs, not expecting an answer.

"Yes?" I whisper back—nervous, "lead the way."

He grins, then steps up to the mic, the hush falling with a physical weight. The band at the edge of the stage peters out mid-carol; the toddlers stop wrestling over snowballs. In that suspended second, it's just Brayden and the crowd and me, standing by his side, heart ricocheting off my ribs like a pinball. "Evening, everyone," he says, voice steady and sure, with just enough Montana drawl to sound right. "For those few who don't know me, I'm Brayden James, Pastor of Grace Hollow." He pauses as the crowd responds with a, "Good Evening", then continues, "First off, can we give a round of applause to the volunteers who got Main Street cleared and made tonight happen?" He gestures, and there's an immediate cheer, a whoop from the snowplow crew, a ripple of gratitude that warms the space like a bonfire.

He waits until the noise dies, then continues. "Some of you know, but most of you probably don't—this is the first festival in a long time where the community has actually grown. Not just in numbers, but in how we care for each other. I've seen more casseroles delivered and more driveways shoveled this week than in the last five years combined." There's a laugh, the sound of people seeing themselves in his words.

"Tonight, before we light the tree, I want to take a second to recognize the heart of Maple Ridge: all the people who show up. Whether you're a member of Grace Hollow, or just here in town for the fireworks and the funnel cakes, you're the reason this place is special."

He closes his eyes for a moment, letting the murmurs quiet before he begins to speak again. Then, with a gentle, resonant voice, he says, "Heavenly Father, we thank You for gathering us here in the heart of Maple Ridge, for the gift of community, and for the joy of this Christmas season. Lord, You have shown us that Your love knows no bounds, that even in our mistakes, even in our wondering, You offer us second chances." He pauses, letting the words sink in, then continues, voice steady and full of warmth. "Father, we pray for hearts to forgive and be forgiven. Teach us to see one another not through our pasts, but through the hope of redemption You offer us each day. May this festival be more than music and lights, may it be a reminder that Your love is present in every laugh, every hug and every shared moment. Bless this Christmas festival, Lord. Bless our families and our friends. In the name of Your Son, Jesus Christ, we pray." "Amen," the crowd echoes, their voices mingling in the night as snowflakes drift lazily down, catching the glow of the festive lights.

He pauses, and for a split second, looks at me—really looks, as if all the rest is just preamble for this moment. "There's someone else who came back this week, someone who reminded us that you can always come home, no matter how long you've been gone, or how hard the road was. Would you join me in welcoming Tess Somerset?"

I freeze for half a heartbeat. Then, as if my legs remember what to do, I step up next to him, blinking against the white- hot attention of everyone I've ever known. The hand-off is seamless; he gives my fingers a squeeze and then lets go, leaving me alone with the mic and my own, ragged breath.

I look out at the crowd, and for the first time, I see more hope than suspicion in their faces. I spot my parents, standing arm in arm near the cider tent, Mom clutching a tissue and Dad watching like he's about to grade my performance.

I clear my throat, voice barely above a whisper. "Hi," I start. There's a scattered chuckle—people are rooting for me, or at least not against me. I let the warmth carry me forward. "I don't have a speech. I'm not even sure why Brayden thought I'd want to talk. But I do want to say this...coming back to Maple Ridge was the scariest thing I've done in a long time. Not because of the blizzards, or the pageants, or even the memories. It's scary to let people see the real you, especially when you're not sure you deserve it."

I swallow, looking for the next words. "But if there's one thing this week taught me, it's that nobody here is perfect. Not one. And sometimes, all you need is a little grace...a little time, a second chance, or, in my case, a second and third and maybe tenth."

The crowd gives a laugh, and even I smile. I can see Nancy in the front row, nodding as if she's hearing her own sermon.

"So, what I really want to say is thank you. For letting me come back. For letting me try again. And for giving me a chance to help, instead of just hiding. And for giving me the grace I needed to find my way back." I look over at my father, then back at the faces below. "I'll be staying in Maple Ridge. Starting soon, I'll be joining Somerset Family Medical, working alongside my dad. And I can't wait to take care of you the way you've taken care of me."

There's a stunned second, as if the announcement needs to circle the block before landing. Then, from somewhere near the back, comes a single whoop—followed by clapping, followed by a rising wall of applause. The sound builds, echoes off the snowbanks, swells until it drowns out every trace of the old, brittle shame. I glance at Brayden, who is beaming like a little kid who just got exactly what he wished for.

He slides an arm around my waist, and for a long moment, the two of us just stand there, absorbing the noise, letting it patch the last of the old wounds.

When we step down from the stage, it's like walking through a tunnel of light. People stop to shake my hand, to hug Brayden, to thrust home-baked cookies or invitation cards or half-melted snowmen in our general direction. The town that once specialized in rumor has shifted gears; now they want to claim us, celebrate us, remind us that home isn't just a place you land— it's a place you build, every day, with every choice to forgive and move forward.

As the music starts up again (a rendition of "Hark! the Herald Angels Sing" that would bring a tear to even the most jaded ER doc), I feel the first flakes of new snow dust my hair. Brayden turns to me, brushing the dusting from my coat.

"You did it," he whispers, voice as close and sure as a heartbeat. "You're home."

We walk together, hand in hand, through the thrumming core of the festival. The lights blur above us, the snow thickens, and behind us, our footprints lay a double trail in the new powder: side by side, weaving a path no storm or history can erase. I let the world fill up with hope and music, knowing that I don't need to run from anything anymore. I only want to see where this story will go.

And if tonight is any indication, it's going to be beautiful.

A Year Later

T he last appointment clears out at 4:40 p.m., a toddler with the world's most impressive snot mustache and a mother who thanks me four times before
she wrangles her winter gear and vanishes into the lobby.
The place goes otherworldly quiet—a small-town clinic
on Christmas Eve, the hum of the fridge in the break room
the only thing refusing to take a holiday. I savor the quiet,
then set to my favorite vice—the tidying of patient charts.

It's a paperless system, technically, but anyone who's
worked rural medicine knows the only thing less reliable
than a county broadband connection is a hospital server
older than a third grader. So I have a hybrid system:
digital entry backed up by color-coded folders, each one
hand-labeled in block letters and stacked with precision
in the file cabinet by the nurse's station.

I'm in the zone, a rare pocket of Type A bliss, when I sense my dad. He slides into the doorway of the glassed-in office. His arms are crossed, his sweater is the same brown he's favored since my childhood, and his mouth is set in that thin line which, in family lexicon, translates as, "I'm pretending to be annoyed but actually bursting with pride." "Most doctors would have closed up by noon," he observes, deadpan. "You planning on a midnight mass for the flu vaccine?"

I slide a chart into its folder, not looking up. "Well Dad, if you'd kept up with the flu shot reminders, half the town wouldn't be here wheezing all winter."

He grunts—a noise that, translated, is equal parts grudging respect and the joy of a good sparring partner. "Did you know it's Christmas Eve?" he asks, stepping in and lowering himself into the ancient, squeaky office chair across from me.

I gesture to the plastic tree in the corner, its fiber-op-tic tips pulsating green and blue under the fluorescent lights. "I picked up on the theme."

He leans forward, elbows on knees. "You don't have to prove yourself every day, you know. Not to me. Not to anyone here." I snap the file drawer shut, a little too loud, and let the silence fill in before answering. "If I stopped proving myself, you'd just start reorganizing all the charts again by blood type, and we both know it."

He gives the smallest of smiles. "Guilty as charged."

We sit like that, across the little room, for a full minute—just letting the day wind down. On the wall behind Dad is a photo of us from my med school graduation: me in a cap and gown, him in the same battered sweater, both of us squinting into the sun. Next to it is a framed printout of the New York Times announcement from my residency, and next to that, a get-well card from Mabel, who signed it "Your Favorite Patient, Don't Tell Nancy."

The air smells like printer ink and faint Lysol, with a chaser of spruce from the electric diffuser someone (me) splurged on last month.

"The office looks good," Dad says at last, his gaze roving the waiting area through the glass. "You've brought more life into it than I ever managed."

"Is that your subtle way of saying I overdecorate?" I ask, flicking my eyes at the collection of cards, the silver garland looped over the reception desk, and the candy dish that's been refilled three times in as many days.

His expression goes wry. "Nope. Never."

I laugh, the sound catching me off guard, and then I push back from the desk, hands finally idle for the first time in eight hours. "You ready to get out of here?" I ask, voice lighter now.

He stands, stretches, and then looks me dead in the eye. "I mean it, Tess. You've done more for this place than I did in the last ten years."

"Maybe that's because you finally have some help," I say, and the moment hangs, real and close.

He nods, as if accepting a diagnosis. "For which I am very thankful for."

I step into the exam room to grab my things and slip off the white coat—officially on loan from the practice, but I'd be lying if I said it didn't make me feel exactly as cool as I imagined at age nine. I swap it for my true uniform, an aggressively festive sweater with a cartoon reindeer, complete with a real, battery- operated nose that lights up in a pulsing red. (A gift from Holly, our only nurse, who threatens to call OSHA if I take it off before New Year's.)

When I emerge, Dad is waiting by the back door, fiddling with the lock and humming the first four bars of "O Come, O Come, Emmanuel." He's got a box under one arm—leftover charts for remote entry, the man will never change—and his other hand is clutching a thermos.

"You want a ride, or is your boyfriend picking you up?" he asks, eyebrows arched to the absolute ceiling.

The word makes me blush, which is idiotic, but it does. "He's not my boyfriend," I say, the way a kid says, "He's not my dad's favorite" about the family dog. "He's my..."

As if summoned on queue, Brayden's pickup appears out the back window, rumbling into the snowy lot with its headlights winking through a fine haze of flurries. He parks with surgical precision, inches from the curb, then hops out, blue flannel and denim like a Norman Rockwell update.

Dad watches through the glass, then turns to me. "You could do worse," he mutters, with an unmistakable tone of sarcasm. Brayden slaps the snow off his boots before entering, then pops the door open with a gust of December air. "Evening, Doc," he calls, eyes going from Dad to me with the ease of someone who's been running this play for a year.

"Evening, Pastor," Dad returns, the words as smooth as butter off a knife.

I pull my bag onto my shoulder, making a show of zipping it up just as Brayden sidles up next to me.

"Ready to escape?" he whispers, like he's offering me a ticket out of prison.

"More than ready," I reply. "But you're driving, which means I'm expecting actual heat this time."

He feigns insult. "The heater works just fine if you treat her right."

Dad snorts, hands already on the lock. "Treat her right? If you treat my daughter like you treat your truck, you might not make it to the spring."

"Hey now, this is premium Ford engineering," Brayden retorts, straight-faced. "She just has quirks."

I roll my eyes, but it's impossible not to smile.

Dad opens the door and ushers us out into the crunch of snow and the faint, sharp scent of woodsmoke that always drifts over from Main Street this time of year. As we head toward the pickup, Dad calls out, "Pastor—don't be late for Christmas breakfast tomorrow. Her mother's making her special cinnamon rolls, and you know she'll never let you forget if you miss it."

Brayden turns, arm around my shoulders, and grins back at Dad. "Wouldn't dream of it, Doc."

We pile into the pickup. The heater wheezes to life with all the determination of a seventy-year-old marathon runner, and the cab fills with an odd but comforting mix of exhaust, cold, and the lingering peppermint from the candy dish.

Through the window, I see Dad locking up, his silhouette hunched against the wind, then watch as he pauses to look back at us. His hand rises in a brief, almost embarrassed wave, and I feel the pulse of everything that's changed, and can't help but feel warm inside.

Brayden puts the truck in gear, and as we bump out onto the snow-packed road, he glances over and asks, "Ready for tonight?"

I lean back against the seat, warmth settling into my toes as I smile to myself. Outside, the Montana sky stretches wide and brilliant, the snow-draped mountains standing quiet and sure—like the world, for once, has found its peace.

We drive slowly through Maple Ridge, snow feathering down in soft, hypnotic sheets, the whole town lit up like the inside of a Christmas snow globe. Every storefront window is crowded with garland, glowing reindeer, and enough tinsel to deflect a solar flare. The hardware store has that giant inflatable Santa still clinging to the roof, arms flailing in the wind. There are wreaths on every door and not a single stretch of curb without some kind of lights strung, even the ones that never light up the rest of the year.

Main Street isn't busy—half the town's at home prepping for tomorrow, the other half already parked at the church—but the world feels alive and waiting, like the best possible kind of suspended animation. In the warmth of the pickup, I let myself be hypnotized by it. For once, I don't feel like an outsider pressing my nose to the glass. I'm exactly where I'm meant to be.

Brayden steers with one hand resting on the wheel, the other stretching lazily across the seat between us.

He's humming along to the radio—Bing Crosby's "White Christmas"—and glancing over occasionally, as if making sure I'm still real.

"It's funny," he says, breaking the trance, "but I think I prefer Maple Ridge at night." He nods out at the empty sidewalks, the storefronts bright against the endless white. "It's like the whole world vanished...just so we can have it all to ourselves."

I watch a trio of kids dart past the pharmacy, their faces bright with cold and pure sugar from whatever they scored at the festival. "That, or the Christmas lights are the only thing holding Main together after 5 p.m.," I say.

He grins, the dimple I always forget about until I see it catching at the corner of his mouth. "Either way, it works."

We drift past the diner. It's closed for the holiday, the "Best Pie in Montana" sign only barely legible under a drift of snow. I think of how many times we'd ducked in there as kids, plotting world domination or, later, hiding out from whatever crisis we'd caused. It's the first place I ever told Brayden a real secret—the only place I ever cried in public. There's something about the sight of it now, dark but familiar, that makes my heart twist.

"Remember when we used to fake stomachaches just to skip gym class and eat fries in the back booth?" Brayden asks, catching my glance.

"I remember you dared me to chug three packets of ketchup and I did it. You chickened out and blamed it on your allergies."

He laughs, warm and deep. "I had allergies. You just had something to prove."

"Yeah. Okay," I reply, rolling my eyes.

He turns onto Church Road, the tires crunching over fresh powder. The sign for Grace Hollow is covered in frost, but you can see the new hand-painted banner peeking underneath: "CHRISTMAS EVE CANDLELIGHT 7 P.M. ALL ARE WELCOME."

The closer we get to the church, a few cars line the street, each one dusted in snow, some with windows already fogged from the warmth inside. Brayden pulls into the parking lot, the pickup coming to a stop and idling while we both watch cars and trucks pulling into the parking lot. The church itself is aglow, every window a watercolor of stained glass and candlelight.

Brayden turns down the radio, lets the engine tick in the quiet. He looks at me, then out at the church, then back again.

"This feels different," he says, the words hanging in the air between us.

"Different how?" I ask, but I already know.

He looks up, thinking. "Last year, I thought I was just—patching things up. Filling the gap until you found some-place better. I didn't think...well, I didn't think we'd be here again.

Doing this together. Planning our future."

I glance down at our hands—his sitting still on the seat and mine still shaky from the adrenaline rush of the day, but already reaching for his.

I squeeze his fingers. "I didn't think so either," I say, the words coming out honest, raw.

He smiles, but it's shy this time. "Speaking of fu-tures—how much trouble are we in if your mom insists on making her five- cheese casserole for the rehearsal dinner?"

"Tons," I reply. "She's already started hoarding the weird block cheese from Billings. I think there's a secret bunker in the basement."

He makes a face. "I swear, your family is trying to kill me."

I laugh, watching his breath fog up the cab. "She says she's only trying to fatten you up. You don't eat enough."

We sit for another beat, letting the engine hum lull us into a cocoon of comfort. Outside, the first real crowd starts to filter into the church. There's a line of candles along the walkway, each flame a tiny orange miracle in the blue dark. I watch them flicker, and I think about how many times I tried to run away from this place, only to find my way back, finally.

Brayden glances at me, his eyes catching mine in that way that always makes me feel like he can see through to the very last layer.

"Are you nervous?" he asks, voice low.

I shake my head. "No. Not about the service. Not about any of it."

He raises an eyebrow. "Not even about getting married to the town's most notorious pastor?"

"Not even a little," I say, and it's true. "If I can survive your sermons, I can survive anything."

He laughs. "I can't begin to tell you how thankful I am."

I don't say anything, I just leave my hand on his, feeling the warmth of his skin.

The world outside is all anticipation—people standing in the parking lot, lights blazing from parking cars, the sound of distant laughter echoing over the snow. But inside the truck, it's just the two of us and the warmth that fills the space.

I look at the church, then at Brayden, and I'm actually not afraid of what comes next.

He squeezes my hand, then leans over and kisses the top of my head, the gesture so simple and right that it knots up every nerve in my body and then lets them all go.

"Ready?" he asks. "Let's do this," I say.

We push out into the night together, hand in hand, and walk toward the doors and the life that's finally, truly ours.

There's an old joke that Grace Hollow used to be held together with prayer, potluck, and stubbornness—but after last year's storm damage, the congregation decided it was time for some improvements. Now the foyer gleams with soft lighting and polished wood floors, the kind of warmth that comes from fresh paint and a community determined to start fresh. The air hums with quiet conversation, especially around the new coffee station in the corner, where people cluster with steaming cups and easy laughter. There's a real tree in the foyer this year—my handiwork— decked with hand-knit angels and a battalion of candy canes that already look half-raided by sneaky Sunday Schoolers. The chair rail glows with led lights, winding toward the sanctuary where a brass trio is rehearsing "What Child Is This," soft and hesitant and exactly right.

Brayden does his pre-service thing with minimal fuss—testing the wireless mic, checking the script for the order of service, and greeting the volunteers with a handshake and a word of encouragement. I do mine—checking the aisles for stray programs, lighting the votives in the windows, making sure hymnals are in every pew. We fall into a rhythm that's comfortable, almost rehearsed. We move around each other the way people do when they've shared years of tight spaces and inside jokes and the absolute certainty that nobody else will ever alphabetize the candle wicks or color-code the tea selection quite the same way.

I straighten up the candles by the altar, then step back to admire the stage. It's transformed: pine garlands loop between the rafters, the cloth hanging from the cross changed to a deep velvet blue, and the side aisles lined with hundreds of votives. It's beautiful, lively and full of anticipation.

From the back, Brayden calls, "You missed one," and I glance up to see him pointing to a single unlit candle on the third window ledge.

I raise an eyebrow. "That's by design. Fire marshal's orders." He grins and crosses the room to meet me. As we stand together at the front, looking out over the rows of pews, I realize with a smile that I thought I'd checked every votive battery. *Apparently not.*

"This feels right," he says at last, his voice a low rumble that blends into the hush of the sanctuary.

I nod. "It really does. I mean, both of us in church together, voluntarily?"

He slips an arm around my waist. "Honestly, I thought you'd end up running the whole ER in New York before returning to this." He looks at me, and the warmth in his eyes almost undoes me. "This is better than anything I ever prayed for."

I laugh, but it's soft and full of all the things I don't have words for. "You know, when I first came back, I thought Maple Ridge was just a holding pen for broken people. Now I can't imagine wanting to be anywhere else."

He kisses my cheek, then steps away to adjust the star above the nativity scene—one of those battery-lit jobs that always tilts to the left no matter how you set it. He frowns at it, nudging it a little, then laughs. "Remember last year?" he asks, hand still on the creche. "The blizzard knocked the power out, and we held together the whole pageant with duct tape and zip-ties?"

I wince. "Don't remind me. I still have nightmares about my dad as Joseph."

He gives me a sideways look. "I spared you that. You saved Christmas. And you managed not to burn the place down. That's impressive."

"High praise from the resident holy man," I shoot back, straightening one of the baby Jesus dolls in the manger. "You know, I used to think you'd never come back to church...because of our past."

He grins, the old cocky Brayden for a flash. "Yeah, God brought me back kicking and screaming. But look at you now, too. Dr. Somerset, upstanding citizen, lighting candles for Jesus and everything."

I shake my head. "I'm marrying a pastor. God has a sense of humor, that's for sure."

He comes over, leans in close so only I can hear. "It's the only way He gets through to stubborn types like us."

Before I can answer, the doors open and the first trickle of early birds makes their way in: the same cluster of elderly ladies who ran every bake sale and every prayer circle since the Eisenhower administration. They spot me and converge, peppering me with greetings and air kisses, each one inspecting my sweater as if it's a pageant sash.

"You look radiant, dear," one says, pinching my arm. Another leans in, "So good to see your smiling face again." A third— Mabel, of course—simply wraps me in a hug and whispers, "I just knew it would work out."

I can't help but blush, but it's a good feeling. The nervousness that used to choke me in rooms like this is gone, replaced by something new. Belonging. Maybe even love.

The church fills up quickly. By six forty-five, the pews are a patchwork of families, old friends, and the odd townie who just likes Christmas music. There are kids in pajamas, couples in matching scarves, a few out-of-town relatives taking in the spectacle with the kind of wary awe reserved for tourist attractions. The whole place glows.

Brayden and I slip out for a minute, escaping the crowd for a last circuit through the vestibule. The air outside the sanctuary is quiet and a little cold, the entryway empty except for the tree and the muted echo of carols from inside.

We pause under the arch that's been hung with a garland thick enough to choke a moose, a huge wreath hanging over the center. Music is playing softly from a small outdoor speaker—Matthew West's "The Heart of Christmas." It's a little ridiculous, and I start to laugh, but then Brayden takes my hands and the world just stops.

He brushes the snow from my shoulder, then tucks a loose strand of hair behind my ear. "Merry Christmas," he says.

I smile, barely able to speak. "Merry Christmas."

He grins, then pulls me into a kiss—gentle, unrushed, the kind of kiss that fills up all the empty spaces you never knew you had. For a second, all I can hear is my own heart, the sound of bells starting up somewhere in the distance, and the music swelling from the sanctuary.

We pull apart and walk together back into the church. The bells ring louder, the congregation rising in a sea of red and green and white. Brayden makes his way to the pulpit, I take my seat in the front, and as he starts the service, I look out at the faces shining in the candlelight and I realize just how grateful I am. *Thank you Lord for bringing me home.*

Maybe there's no such thing as a perfect ending. But this? This is the beginning I never knew I was waiting for.

The voices rise, the music pours out into the snowy night, and outside, a fresh dusting of snow turns everything pure and new.

I close my eyes, breathe in the moment, and let the Lord work His Christmas miracle.

THANK YOU

Thank you for joining me in Maple Ridge for Christmas at Grace Hollow and for walking with Tess through her journey of redemption, healing, hope, and homecoming. Her story is not just hers alone. It is a reflection of the greatest story ever told — the story of Christ's coming into our world to bring us forgiveness, peace, joy, and a place to belong.

This season reminds us that no matter where we are in life, we are never beyond the reach of God's redeeming love. He comes into the ordinary, the broken, the lonely places of our hearts to bring light, to heal, and to call us home. My prayer is that this book has been a gentle reminder of that truth for you.

If Tess's journey encouraged or touched you, I would be deeply grateful if you would share your thoughts. Your review on Amazon, Goodreads, or social media are more than words to me — they are blessings. They help others find this story and the message it carries.

May this Christmas season bring you the joy of redemption, the peace of healing, the certainty of hope, and the warmth of coming home.

With gratitude and prayer,
Chad

Acknowledgements

This Christmas season, my heart is full of gratitude.

To Linda Kidd — thank you for editing this story with such care. Your wisdom has been a gift to *Christmas at Grace Hollow*. You also graciously reminded me that I forgot how to make cookies...and that not everything smells like cinnamon.

To my wonderful wife — thank you for your patience through countless hours of writing, revising, and marketing. Your love, support, and prayers are my greatest Christmas blessing.

To my alpha readers — your insight and encouragement have been invaluable. This story is richer because of you.

May the joy of Christmas remind us all that no matter how far we wander, there is always a place to come home to.

With a grateful heart,

Chad

"But the angel said to them, 'Fear not, for behold, I bring you good news of great joy that will be for all the people. For unto you is born this day in the city of David a Savior, who is Christ the Lord.'"

— *Luke 2:10-11*

About the Author

Chad Muessig is a Christian author, chaplain, and worship leader whose stories explore themes of faith, redemption, and hope. A graduate of Word of Life Bible Institute and a career in law enforcement, Chad blends spiritual depth with real-world insight into justice and grace.

His debut novel, *The Sword of the Spirit*, launched a Christian YA fantasy series rooted in biblical truth. His second book, *Christmas at Grace Hollow*, turns that same heart toward a moving Christian Christmas romance.

Chad lives in South Jersey with his wife, their five children, and two grandchildren. When he's not writing, he enjoys drawing or driving his gecko green Jeep Gladiator, affectionately named "Preacher."